EDITORIAL REVIEW

Thor's Dragon Rider
Book Two

PURSUIT

"Fans of the Thor's Dragon Rider series will be pleased with *Pursuit* as Kara returns on an urgent mission to track down the trickster god, Loki. With the assistance of Sobek—the brother of Kara's beloved dragon, Elan—Kara must lead a squad of Valkyries into the icy land of Jotunheim, where they are tested by danger and treachery." Kelly R., Line Editor, Red Adept Editing

Pursuit

Ebook first published in USA in October 2020 by Cosy Burrow
Books

Ebook first published in Great Britain in October 2020 by Cosy
Burrow Books

www.katrinacopebooks.com

Text Copyright © 2020 by Katrina Cope

Cover Design Copyright © art4artists.com.au

Published by Cosy Burrow Books

ISBN: 9780648766186

❀ Created with Vellum

To my readers - may your life be as happy as the gods &
einherjar after drinking Heidrun's mead.

BLURB

Beware of the company kept. All may not be as it seems.

The threat from Loki's monstrous children prevails, as Odin had predicted. With the trickster father at large, only one path remains—the mother must be sweetened. Perhaps a little chat with a frost giantess will go smoothly, and she will happily control her children, right?

Desperate to delay the onset of Ragnarok, Kara must enter Jotunheim and face the danger of the frost giants to seek Angrboda's help. The outcome could go either way, considering the giantess dislikes all Asgardian gods except for her beloved Loki.

Chapter One

A robust fist slams the table, and I jump. The wooden legs squeak their protest at the force. The muscles on Thor's arm twinge, and every fiber of his being expresses his anger. Gradually, his blue eyes rise to mine, his bushy red eyebrows furrowing together like an angry storm approaching from the horizon.

"What on Asgard were you thinking, Kara? How could you let Loki go?"

I swallow, desperately trying to remove the lump clogging my voice box. "I didn't let him go. I promise. I was only releasing him for a moment so he could heal Elan. Nothing else was working, and she… she…" I take a staggered breath, and my lip quivers. "Was dying." My shoulders cave.

His thunderous eyebrows separate slightly as a flash of understanding travels through his eyes. He expels a loud breath. "I understand you needed to save your dragon. I like Elan. I would miss her greatly. But this is Loki." He pushes off from the table and paces. "How could you let Loki out?" The god of thunder pauses, and his eyes land on me again. "There must have been another way you could have healed her." He resumes his pacing, clasping his hands behind his back. "And you've waited this long to let me know!"

I cringe at the disappointment radiating from his body and tone. Guilt twists into my heart, yet deep down, I know I wouldn't have done anything differently.

I flail my arms. "I wanted to let you know. But first, I wanted to at least try to recapture the deceitful god and put him away. I thought I could secure him. I know several of the places he hid before he was captured." I clasp my hands before myself and squeeze tightly. "I thought maybe he would go back to them. I hoped I could return him before anybody would even notice he was missing. I've been searching for him ever since I knew he had bailed."

Thor grunts and slams a fist against a marble wall. The hall is empty, leaving us to have the conversation in private, which was what I hoped when I asked Thor to meet me here to confess my error. Odin's capability to run Asgard remains stilted as he gathers his strength. Even so, his son hasn't been giving me an easy time over my error, and I know I deserve it.

"That's a whole week! We could have helped you search for him. A whole week he's had to escape and blend into his surroundings or flee to another realm." His boots' hard soles clack against the marble floor, silencing when he slumps into a chair next to the throne. His elbow digs into an armrest as he props his head in his hand. After a moment, he slams against the backrest and scratches his bushy red beard. "Loki has caused enough trouble in Asgard. He's probably gathering his forces, getting ready to start another battle. Vanir! He could even be coercing his children."

I rub my upper arm. "I thought his children were the ones causing havoc because Loki had been captured and restrained. Maybe now, we can go to his children and tell them that he's free and they don't need to attack Asgard anymore."

Thor runs a hand through his red hair and struggles when his fingers get caught in the strands. "I like your train of thought, but I don't think his children are that understanding. For one, I know we cannot negotiate or reason with the Midgard Serpent." He loosens his fingers and relaxes his arm on the armrest. "Two, Fenrir is on the borderline. His agitation grows every day. And three, Hel takes pleasure associating with the unworthy dead. In my eyes, that doesn't indicate a pleasant personality." He runs his fingers along the grain of the wooden chair. "Let's anticipate that we sort this mess out before Odin regains his strength and goes back to Mimir's well."

My cheeks turn clammy. I don't need Odin finding out about Loki's escape. As much as I've let Thor down, I know he's more understanding than Odin would ever be. Even so, the disappointment falling from Thor's shoulders causes my heart to sink into the floor. The only way I can look him in the face is by remembering why I did this in the first place. I could never have stood around doing nothing when my loyal dragon was dying. In fact, I couldn't have done nothing if *any* of my friends were in that position.

I hold my head high, certain I followed my moral beliefs. "I will continue my search for him. I promise. My intention was never to set him free. He escaped when I was distracted by my distress and then excitement when Elan's health improved." My feet automatically splay into position, ready for a fight, instinctively displaying eagerness to act. I gaze directly into Thor's eyes. "I will recapture him again, one way or another. He should be captured for the trouble he caused." The image of Loki stripped to his underwear and strung up flashes into my mind. "But do you really think he should be contained the way he was? To me, it seems excessive to have his bare skin exposed to a serpent's searing venom."

The edges of Thor's mouth quirk as he appears deep in thought. "It wouldn't be my idea of punishment. But you have seen what my father is like when somebody upsets him. He can be quite unreasonable at times."

I huff. "You think? It took me ages to get him to treat wingless Valkyries the same as the winged and to look after the dragons rather than treating them as something to fight against." I rock my weight onto one leg. "The last thing I need right now is for Odin to find out."

Thor's expression is clouded with disappointment and annoyance, which shoots straight at my heart, yet at the same time, understanding barely glimmers in his eyes.

"What do you suggest we do, then?" I ask.

The god tosses his arms out to the sides. "We have to continue to protect Asgard. Fenrir is still angry, although he seems to view the game with the chain as fun. So far, he has broken through every binding the gods have placed around him."

"But is he angry because of his father's capture or something else?"

"I don't know. Tyr can't quite understand why he

has suddenly changed from a cute pup to a large hound with a grudge on his shoulder."

I smirk. "Maybe Loki's children are dealing with the hormones of teenagers."

Filled with disbelief, Thor's eyes level with mine, and I swallow my amusement. Showing disrespect to my understanding leader isn't the best response. He's nothing like his father. He didn't deserve me going behind his back and making things worse. The last thing I should be doing is joking about these things.

I straighten my black fighting leathers and nudge the marble floor with the toe of my boot. "Look. I'm sorry that I have let you down. Although I have to be honest and say that I would do it again if any of my friends were in danger and on the brink of death. Like I said, I never intended for Loki to go free. I had every intention of returning him to where the gods had put him, as much as I disagree with the punishment." I toss my hands high. "But I'm not the ruler of Asgard nor its judge, to uphold the law."

Thor rests back in his chair. "No, you are not. And Loki cannot be left to run free. Until he has served his sentence or learned his lesson."

Worrying my bottom lip, I stare at him with apprehension. "Are you certain that Loki was going against Asgard? I know it's a long shot, but things don't add up."

"I know some things have come to light that may make it appear so." Thor crosses his legs, the leather in his pants squeaking. "But Loki must be recaptured, and then we can discuss what exactly his intentions are." He fixes his eyes on me. "Your actions must be fixed, Kara."

I nod. "How can I make this right?"

"You can find him by whatever means."

"Like what?" I frown. "What do you mean 'by whatever means'?"

Thor's eyebrows push together. "You work it out. If Loki is in Asgard, we'll find him. If you think he's not in this realm and you need to leave Asgard, come back and let me know. In the meantime, I'll warn my close circle to be on alert for any odd behavior. Fix this quickly, or I'll be the laughingstock of the gods."

"But *I* did this!" I exclaim. "Not you."

Thor's glowering eyes are crowded by bushy eyebrows, red and threatening, as he fixes his gaze on me. "Yes. But your actions reflect on me. I'm the one held responsible for them."

Chapter Two

My head buzzes with an electric charge. Thoughts dart through my mind, of what was covered in my meeting with Thor. Trying to keep up with the shape-shifting god's mischievous doings was going to be difficult. Blessed with a life of immortality, he's had many years to perfect his twisted ways and betrayals. I, on the other hand, am only a youth. Even though Valkyries live for a very long time, my life has only begun, hopefully. Glancing over my shoulder, I gaze up at the palace windows, spotting the room of the leader of Asgard, and I cringe. If Odin finds out about this, my life might be considerably shorter.

Rapidly, I skim the steps, keen to see Elan. A while has passed since I've displeased the gods. After wingless Valkyries were deemed equal to their winged counterparts, I've been settled and keen to serve Asgard under Thor's instruction. It would be a

shame to lose it all. I've worked hard for my achieve-
ment of serving under Thor and changing Odin's
mindset over wingless Valkyries and the dragon
alliance. Now, I need to work equally hard to keep it.
I hope Loki has remained in Asgard. He would be
easier to find. Then again, his ability to transform
into any creature or being is going to make that a
difficult task, let alone his ability to travel to any of
the nine realms. If he has left Asgard, my task could
be nearly impossible.

I pass the hall of Valhalla, and a gust of wind
pushes me from behind. The rustling of leaves grasps
my attention. I realize I'm not far from the World
Tree, and the sound reminds me of the terrible little
squirrel I met on Midgard. If anybody knows where
Loki is, it would be Ratatoskr. To be good at his job,
he would have to be able to find just about anyone.

Taking a detour, I head toward the trunk of
Yggdrasil. Maybe I can get the squirrel's attention
and ask him.

I scan the branches of the tree towering over me
and forking into smaller limbs covered by leaves. I'm
so focused on finding Ratatoskr that I stumble over a
rock and struggle to right myself. Asgard is such a
rocky, hard place. After having seen Midgard, I'm
surprised we've survived here for so long, a feat
accomplished only by harvesting food from other

realms. It's strange to think that the gods' realm relies on the lands of humans to survive.

I travel through the area where Elan and Thor held their eating competition only days ago, surprised how things have changed for Elan and me in just a couple of days. Merriment and joy have twisted into catastrophe and strife. The Valhalla hall is quiet. The day is early, and the warriors most likely training. The einherjar fill each day with perfecting battle skills to combat Ragnarok, celebrating their efforts by night.

The noise of trickling liquid travels through the leaves of Yggdrasil, and passing under the branches, I follow the sound. The trickling falls silent, and a furry brown face peers at me through the green leaves. A long tongue sticks out and wraps around the leaves before the jaw clamps and chews noisily.

"Heidrun. There you are," I say as I stroke the bridge of her nose.

Her lips smack together as she chews the broken greenery. With more trickling sounds, golden fluid pours out of her udder into a large bowl.

"You've done well. Your mead looks exceptionally good today. The bowl is over half full. The einherjar will be pleased tonight."

She pushes her head into the rub I give her behind an ear, and she bleats.

"Good job for working so hard for the warriors."

I smile to myself. If the warriors didn't have her mead, there would be protests. My thoughts turn to Thor, and I wince. He will most likely miss the celebration tonight, probably spending his time trying to recapture my mistake.

The rough bark of Yggdrasil sends vibrations through my fingers as I trace the grooves, searching for a hole in the trunk. The place that Ratatoskr would exit to visit this area must be nearby. My knowledge of the squirrel is low, although I assume he travels the different realms through holes and branches of the World Tree. Surely, he would have looked for a warrior at some stage, meaning there should be evidence that the squirrel has exited here to visit this area.

Slowly, I circle the trunk, feeling the vibrations up my arm from the coarse bark scraping against my skin. Unable to find a hole, I slap the side of the trunk with my palm. The sound is barely audible, so I knock on the surface with my fist. Frustration shrouds me when my knuckles burn from the impact, yet the sound remains too soft even for my ears. After grabbing a rock from the ground, I smash it against the bark, only slightly satisfied when it creates a more audible sound, yet after several minutes, the squirrel still doesn't show. I slam the rock against the trunk, calling up the rough surface.

"Ratatoskr!"

I wait, hoping the squirrel has heard. When he doesn't come in a few minutes, I call out again.

"Ratatoskr! Ratatoskr!" I scream.

I'm confident that the whole of Asgard will hear me before this squirrel does.

Waiting, I hope to see a sign of that orange-red face with a black snout and pointy ears. It's not the pleasant company I'm looking for, but the hope that he'll surprise me and help me find Loki. He might be smart enough to know that the devious god needs to be found and punished.

While completing another circle of the trunk, I gaze up into its branches, looking for any sign of that little red face, only to be disappointed. "Ratatoskr!"

Then his little red face pokes through the leaves, landing beady eyes on me, his claws digging into the bark. He scurries down the trunk headfirst, tail pointing to the sky, until he pauses at a fork in a branch not far from my head. Standing on his hind legs, he leans against the tree trunk and crosses his forelegs, blocking some of his white furry chest. As though agitated, he flicks his bushy tail from side to side as he points a little claw at me. "Look at you. You seem pale and down. What happened to you?" Not an ounce of sympathy infuses his voice, the lack of empathy confirmed when he shoves his little paw back into his folded arms.

I waggle my head, making sure the sarcasm flows through my voice. "Nice to see you too!"

"Yeah, yeah. Enough with the niceties. What do you want?" He scratches the back of one ear with a hind foot then leans against the tree trunk as though returning to his favorite stance, his arms crossed.

My eyes narrow. "I was hoping you would help me."

His body language displays a lack of friendliness, and he huffs. "Since when do I help people?"

When I inch closer, he straightens his back, knocking away some of my confidence in my plan, but I press on anyway.

"I was hoping it would be different with me. I thought we've built some rapport."

He pushes off the trunk with his furry elbow and paces the small branch. "Valkyrie, love. I thought you would have learned by now that I have rapport with no one."

Acknowledging his condescending tone, I give a little back. "But you know everyone's location, right? Because, you know, you're the messenger. And to be a good messenger, you'd have to know where everyone is."

He waves a front foot at me. "I can find the receiver eventually. But that doesn't mean I know where they are all the time."

I arch an eyebrow. "So that would mean you would be able to find Loki. Right?"

"Pfft. More than likely." He stops pacing, stands firm, and lifts his chin.

"Then can you tell me where Loki is? Please," I add when his face looks set and unrelenting.

He plants his paws on his hips. "You of all people should know that I don't pass on messages without an insult. And I haven't heard any insults aimed at me laced into your request." Setting his claws on the trunk, ready to climb, he calls over his shoulder. "So I'm going to go now."

"But you're not carrying a message," I protest.

"You have requested something from me. Therefore, the message is for me, and I have refused to accept the message because there is no insult included." His words are painstakingly slow, as though explaining to the simpleminded. He pulls himself up on the trunk, his back legs planted, ready to scurry up.

I reach for him. "Wait!"

He pauses.

Glaring, I retort, "You're nothing more than a rodent."

Ratatoskr lets go of the trunk, landing on the branch. "Please. As if that one hasn't been used before." His claws return to the trunk, hooking deeper.

Dumbfounded, I look at him. He's going to make me work at my insults—something I'm not used to doing. I try my luck. "But isn't that an insult for a squirrel?"

He calls over his furry red shoulder, "Of course it is. But it's definitely not original. It's been used so often I'm used to it. If you want me to carry your insult, think of something original. If only I had a dollar for every time someone used that one. I'd be a rich squirrel… Claws! Even if it was only a dime, I'd still be a rich squirrel." He shakes his head, leveling his beady eyes on me. "Don't you think people have tried to get information from me before, without passing a message? Pfft! What am I? A traitor? Not a chance. You can't use me to find out everyone's secrets." He scurries halfway up the tree.

I call up to him. "Wait! I have an insult for Loki."

He huffs loudly then scurries backward, returning to the branch. His black eyes narrow. "What is it, then? It better be good."

As I pause, my mind whirls, trying to think of something to say. "Tell Loki… that he's a lying, evil, conniving god, and he's a disappointment to Asgard."

Ratatoskr presses his back against the tree and crosses his arms before shaking a claw in my face and tutting. "Didn't you use that one last time?"

Frowning, I try to remember. My shoulders slump. "I guess I did. But please wait—I'll think of something," I blurt out quickly, attempting to hold the squirrel there. My brain hurts with trying to do something that doesn't come naturally. "All right. Then what about this? Tell Loki... his last act of disappearing was the lowest thing he has done to me yet. I put my trust in him, giving him another chance. Just because he helped my dragon doesn't pardon him from his punishment, bestowed by the gods of Asgard. Tell him that he is the lowest scum—that his actions place him underneath the Midgard Serpent in the dregs of the bottom of the ocean floor—a scum that should never see the light of day."

Ratatoskr scratches his cheek. "Hmm. I guess that'll do. He might be insulted by that... Maybe." He scurries up the tree, his bushy tail disappearing within the leaves of the World Tree.

"Tell Loki that he needs to bring his butt back here!" I yell.

Chapter Three

M y mind whirls as I try to work out my own intentions, gazing at the spot where the fluffy tail disappeared. I've confused myself. Seeing that Ratatoskr didn't cooperate and tell me where Loki was, I pulled at strings, desperate to get Loki back. But when I think about the insult I sent, I don't know what it will achieve. Loki won't give himself up and return to Asgard to be enslaved deep beneath the palace. I guess I was just saying whatever came to mind at the time.

My shoulders slump in defeat, and I tear my sight away from the tree, wondering what to do next. This isn't news I want to deliver to Thor. I need to create some hope and good news to rectify what I did to save Elan.

Slowly, I trudge down the hill and across the rocky plains, alert as I scan the landscape between the rocky mountains and the academy where I left

Elan. Although Elan is recovering, she still has a lot of healing to do before she regains her energy and strength. The magic that the lava monster infused in her wounds was potent. I'm glad that I have access to an accomplished healer like Anita so that I can leave my dragon in her care while cleaning up my mess.

Within a few hundred yards of the academy, several wingless Valkyries are mounting dragons on an open plain. I recognize the dragons. They were once chained in the mountain, enslaved by Odin and the academy for practicing warfare. A shiver runs down my spine. Those weren't pleasant times. At least the dragons, once sacrificed for the alliance between the dragons and Asgardians, are no longer being mistreated.

The dragons, once mounted by Valkyries, lunge into the sky, and my heart warms. My bond with Elan and my relationship with Eingana had a hand in the change of attitude. Only a couple years ago, wingless Valkyries were treated as slaves, while dragons were injured by the winged Valkyries as they practiced their fighting skills against the magnificent beasts. Now, the dragons that used to be held captive have agreed to stay and work as the wings and fighting companions of the wingless Valkyries.

One of the young Valkyries from the academy leans forward, her long black plait falling down the back of her black fighting leathers. She strokes her dragon in the soft spot under its scales along the back of its neck. I recognize the yellow dragon as one of the babies that had been taken by Loki.

The rider cuddles into the dragon, and from my own experience, I imagine the sharp points of the scales digging into her skin. Even so, as she rests against them, her expression is soft and caring, as though she is cuddling the softest animal in the realms.

A warmth grows in my stomach. I know that feeling. It's the bond between dragon and Valkyrie—a connection I've shared with Elan since I met her.

In many ways, the yellow dragon breed is a similar build to the emperor dragon, Elan's breed, yet slightly smaller and less intimidating. The other dragons are also different—each color having a different build. In front of me, the small group consists of one of each of the dragon breeds that have bonded with my friends. A smaller blue dragon, just like Naga, stands next to the yellow. Its big blue eyes survey its surroundings, and it furls and unfurls its wings several times, showing off white stars on the undersides of its wings when it stretches them to the sky. The white stars seem to help this breed of dragon blend better into the blue skies when seen from underneath. The next dragon in line is a red. Intimidating, fiery red eyes survey the area. These dragons have a hump in the middle of their torsos resembling a camel's. It's an odd shape for a dragon and probably slows it down with the interrupted aerodynamics, but the glaring red eyes alone would make prey want to run in the opposite direction. The last dragon in line is brown, just like Drogon. The breed's size is thinner than many of the others, and the wings are attached to the front legs, making it an excellent glider, a talent resembling a bat's. Any opponent is often scared away just by looking at the array of horns covering the head and upper neck, almost as thick as a porcupine's quills. No emperor dragons like Elan are around. That breed is larger and lays fewer eggs, making it rarer. The dragons and Valkyries practice taking off and landing. The chance to learn how to stay on the back of a dragon is a privilege I missed out on, and I certainly didn't have a saddle when I first rode Elan.

Pressing forward, I round the corner of the towering mountain splitting the academy away from the dragon training ground. My happy thought of the dragons and Valkyries bonding is heightened when I spot my golden emperor dragon lying with her head resting on her front feet and her eyes closed. She looks peaceful, curled up with her tail wrapped around the front of her body. The light beautifully bathes the golden scales of my favorite dragon in the world. All the distress of the morning is shoved to the back of my mind as I observe her body, which looks robust again. Her sharp horns somehow appear unthreatening even though she is from the breed of the most ferocious dragons in the area.

I plunk down next to her nostrils and place a hand softly on her snout. I can't help touching her even though I don't want to disturb her rest. She needs all she can get. Weakness plagues her robust form. The only thing that keeps me going is that she seems to be healed of the magical poison from the lava monster.

Gently, I slide my hand down her snout to the soft part of her nostril and inject some of my magic's strength into her, hoping to speed her process. A hot puff of steam exits her nostrils, warming my legs through my black leather pants, and I gaze up to her eyes. Her eyelids slit slightly wider than her pupils— enough for her to peer through. Seeing her alert and responding to me again is a relief. Thinking she was going to die was too much to bear. And as I said to Thor, even though I know getting Loki out without permission was wrong, I would do it again to save my best dragon friend.

Her telepathic voice hums in my mind. *Hey, you.*

I smile. "Hey to you too. It's good to see you in the land of the living."

Her large mouth expands with a yawn, and she stretches her front legs, narrowly missing me. *I'm not quite there yet, but I'm feeling a bit better today. Just really, really tired. I feel like my mind is stuck in dreamland.*

"I can imagine. You have been through a lot." I rub my palms together, regathering any magic and letting it well between my palms and fingertips. "I hope this helps." With her soft nose between my palms, I again release into her all the power I've gathered. "Does this help?"

The edges of her mouth tilt up slightly, and she yawns again. *Ever so slightly.*

My forehead furrows. "Really? That was as much energy as I could give you in one hit."

Disappointment swamps me, and I slump. If that's all my entire magic energy does when she's feeling better, it's no wonder my injecting energy and healing power into her when she was really sick didn't do anything.

She nudges me lightly with her nose. *You have to remember you're a lot smaller than me. In case you haven't noticed, I have a much bigger form.* Her words are sluggish and her speech slow, almost like she's drunk. She rests her chin on her front talons again. *It would take a lot of your energy to make any difference to this form.*

Sitting tall, I say, "Yes, you are big. I certainly can't carry you when you're injured."

Unusual sounds exit her mouth, almost like she's giggling but too tired to execute it properly. She garbles, *That would be a sight to see.*

I smile, picturing it in my mind. "Yes, it would be rather funny. Although I don't think you would be able to see me."

Elan lets out a big puff of warm air. "No. You would be squashed." She chuckles.

I chuckle with her, resting a hand against her scales, unable to resist the urge to touch her after the ordeal of thinking I'd lose her. "It's so good to see you getting some of your humor back again. You must be feeling better."

I'm getting there. Her eyes close for a moment as though chuckling had taken too much energy. I play with some loose rocks circling my body, flicking them in different directions.

Her voice enters my head again. *What's up? You look sad and worried.*

"Yes and no. I'm glad you're looking better, and I wouldn't do anything differently, but I'm in a lot of trouble. Thor is extremely upset with me, and I can't work out how to fix this mess I've created."

Is he disappointed in you?

I nod. "I don't really blame him. I did kind of let Loki go. Definitely not on purpose."

Elan's mind seems to sharpen, and she lifts her head slightly to stare at me with astonished eyes. *Does he know why you did it?*

"Yes, and I believe he understands, but I still need to find Loki somehow to make it better. He must be brought back. Thor's glad that you're better and that Loki could help you. I think the only reason he hasn't told Odin yet is because I brought him out to heal you." I flick another rock aside. "So hopefully, I can find Loki and get him to return before Odin knows anything about this."

What about Loki's children? Won't they settle down now that Loki is free? She momentarily sounds a little more coherent.

"You would think so, except the Midgard Serpent is still causing trouble, and Fenrir is still angry. Who knows if Hel is going to send any more of those lava monsters or something similar from her realm?"

Was it Hel who sent the monster?

"We believe so." I hug my knees to my chest. "Where else would a monster filled with lava come from? From Fenrir and the Midgard Serpent's actions, either they don't know Loki is free, or they don't care and want to wage war on Asgard anyway.

Although I must admit, other than being a little grumpy, Fenrir hasn't really done anything yet."

Have the gods managed to secure him in a chain yet?

I get up and stretch my legs. "No. Fenrir still breaks every chain they make. Even the one that the gods designed, which needed several of them to carry it over and place it around his neck. He's one powerful hound, and I'm not surprised the gods are afraid of him."

Then perhaps you should go see their mother. Maybe you can ask her to control her children and get them to settle down.

"But that's not finding Loki." I wipe my hands over the backside of my pants.

True. But maybe the mother will know where Loki is. Even if she doesn't, if she can control her children and stop them from attacking Asgard and Midgard, what are you going to lose? That way, Odin will still be happy with you if he finds out about Loki's escape.

Deep in thought, I push my mouth out to one side. "That might work. I must discuss this with Thor. He said he didn't want me to leave Asgard without telling him where I was going first."

Chapter Four

E lan's right. This plan is a long stretch, but it's all I have to work with. The mother might have control over the children, and she might know where Loki is. Even so, the trip could be dangerous. The last I heard, the mother lives in her native realm, deep in Jotunheim, the land of the frost giants. That's another reason I need to confide in Thor. Perhaps he will come with me.

Standing tall against the wall of the entrance, Den guards the doors to the hall. "Greetings, Kara. You're back so soon?" His blue eyes are serene as he surveys me.

I stick my head into the room where I met with Thor. It's empty. "Yes. I need to speak to Thor. Do you know where he went?"

"I believe he's practicing his battle skills against the other gods and einherjar."

My apprehension dulls. To know that Thor has

had the opportunity to work off some of his frustration since we talked is a relief. A solid workout, especially practice fighting, cures all kinds of annoyance and gives the mind reprieve. "Is that in the usual sparring spot?" I ask.

"I believe so."

"Thank you."

Grunts of effort synchronize with the clanging of swords before I can see the sparring ground. I pause at the edge of the battlefield, gazing down into the open area resembling an arena, and watch the gods and warriors battle. Several pairs of warriors are scattered throughout the flat ground, and I search each sparring couple until I spot Thor in the distance.

A gruff voice sounds behind me. "What are you doing here, Valkyrie?"

Taken aback, I spin around to face Fenrir. His lips pull back, showing off his vast display of sharp canines—the expression looks more like a snarl than a smile.

"Oh, Vanir!" I hold a hand over my heart. "What are you doing sneaking up on me?" Since the hound has been more irritable these days, I lean toward caution and retreat slightly. I'm not keen on a confrontation with Loki's animal child.

His large brown eyes stare at me in a way that

makes the skin on my neck crawl. "I could ask you the same thing."

Not for one moment do I take my eyes off him. "I was looking for Thor." I motion toward the sparring field with my hand. "And I've found him." I try a friendly approach. "Thanks for asking, Fenrir. I'm glad you would've helped me if you could." I make sure my voice hides all emotions and slowly take another backward step.

His fangs protrude a little more, and I retreat farther before turning to leave and almost sprinting to the sparring field. Casting a last glance over my shoulder, I make sure the massive hound hasn't followed me. I sit on a seat on the edge of the field, mesmerized by Thor's battle skills. I'm not in a hurry to interrupt him. Only on rare occurrences have I had the chance to watch Thor sparring. I'm surprised at how quickly he can move his bulky form.

Moving with strength and assurance, Thor dodges a sword that swings his way. He retaliates with a swipe of his own sword at Balder. The blessed god maneuvers, his shoulder-length blond hair swishing to the side. The strands covering his skin fall away, exposing the radiant glow and kindness expressed on the god's face. No wrinkles of worry line Thor's brother's face as the god of thunder slices his sword across his abdomen. It bounces off his torso without a nick to his skin. The move should have spilled his guts on the ground, but as usual, the promise made by everything to not harm Balder rings true.

It seems like such an unusual request from all things, yet not really. His mother's love must be incredibly strong, and because she holds the power of a goddess, she used it to protect her son. That's a power I wish I possessed, to protect my friends. Then I wouldn't be in this mess in the first place. Yet I am merely a Valkyrie, not a goddess.

Thor jabs his sword at Balder's open side. Once again, the strike is true, but the edges of the sword seem to turn to foam just as it touches the handsome god's body, bouncing off him and leaving him unharmed. Balder shrugs and smiles, light radiating off his well-defined face. His eyes catch mine, and my heart skips a beat. For an instant, I understand where Britta's fascination comes from. I shake my head, clearing the strange sensation.

Balder's distraction makes him too slow to avoid the next strike. I would hate to think what would happen if he lost the gift and things were able to harm him. Then again, if something was able to hurt him, he would probably practice better and dodge anything thrown his way. Balder refocuses on his battle and circles his opponent, turning his back toward me. Thor follows to face Balder, moving into a position to face me. He catches my eye for a split second then brings his sword down, left then right. Balder dodges to the side, missing the strikes. Thor then adjusts his grip and jabs straight at Balder's torso and connects, the tip of his sword bouncing off the bright god's abdomen, and Balder moves to the side, unharmed.

Thor pauses. "Okay. That will do for now." He slides his sword back into its sheath hanging from his belt and marches to my side.

Pushing myself off my seat, I'm greeted by the smell of sweaty leather when a gust of breeze blows from behind Thor.

He wipes an arm across his forehead, removing the sweat trickling into his eyes, his breath slightly uneven and recovering from the spar. "Kara. What is it?"

"I've been talking to Elan." I push my mouth into a straight line. "Well, actually, have been talking to Ratatoskr and Elan."

"Yes." His face is blank, his tone unimpressed.

"Ratatoskr wasn't helpful when I tried to locate Loki. Although I've managed to send an insult. If Loki has any kind of conscience, he'll come back." When disappointment tarnishes Thor's features, I hold up a hand. "I know it's a long shot. But after that, I talked to Elan. She suggested that I go to Jotunheim and talk to Loki's mistress and see if she will help us. Maybe Agrboda will hold her children back from attacking Asgard."

Thor rolls his head back and closes his eyes.

"I-I…" I stammer. "I know it is not impressive, but it's something. Maybe she knows where Loki is, and I can ask her while I'm there."

Thor looks at me, his face softening slightly, almost to the expression he usually held before I broke Loki out. "I doubt it'll work, but it may have potential. At least you should be able to search Jotunheim while you're there."

Slight apprehension travels through me. I had hoped he would offer to accompany me. "Would you like to come? I know this has the potential to be a dangerous mission."

Breath hisses through his nostrils. "I have to stay here, Kara, in case the children attack."

His gaze passes my shoulder and up the hill, and I turn to spot Fenrir, sitting on his hind legs, his gaze fixed on me with narrowed eyes. The hound's scruffy fur shows signs of personal neglect.

Thor continues, "Fenrir's current stance confirms that I need to stay here and make sure the children can't attack Asgard."

The skin on my back crawls as my eyes connect with the large hound's. Facing Thor, I nod.

"Why don't you take your Valkyrie friends and their dragons? Surely if the four of you stick together and keep your heads on, you'll be able to stay out of trouble. You're all trained battle maidens with dangerous dragon allies to help."

"But I can't take Elan." I can hear the disappointment in my own voice.

Thor places a hand on my shoulder, his gaze soft with compassion. "I know you have a special bond with her, but surely there must be another dragon you can ask to go with you. After all, you have managed to make them into our allies."

I groan softly, rolling my shoulders to relieve some tension. "It's not my favorite option, but you're right. I have to find another dragon."

"I have faith in you, Kara. That's why you were sent to help me. You have initiative, and with your trained Valkyrie friends, you should be fine. After all, you've been to the land of the frost giants before." His one eyebrow rises, and I see the loveable brute again.

"Yeah, but it wasn't by choice. It was another of Loki's strange plots."

Thor chuckles. "At least this time you have the opportunity to take some warm clothes."

"Like I had a choice last time," I say sarcastically.

Chapter Five

C ollapsing to my knees next to Elan's face, I rest my head against her snout. She still hasn't moved from the spot next to the academy. "You were right, Elan. Thor wants us to go and visit Angrboda."

She lifts her head to look at me, gently knocking me back. *That's awesome! I'll prepare to leave.* She pushes on her front legs to stand, and her knees buckle, flopping her back to the ground with a grunt.

After squeezing her snout in a hug, I stand. "You're in no shape to come with me. You have to stay. As much as I don't want to go without you, you're not going to make it in your condition."

She narrows her eyes at me. *There's no way I'll let you go alone. I'm coming with you whether you like it or not.*

"I'd love you to come with me, but you're still regaining your energy. You have nowhere near enough to get us there and back."

She lowers her golden eyes to the level of mine and glowers.

Not wanting to see her disappointment, I gaze down at my hands clasped in front of me. "Thor suggested I take another dragon. Do you have any ideas?" I meet her stare. "I don't want to. I'd rather take you."

Her mouth seems to droop at the sides, and sadness fills her golden-brown eyes. I rest my hands on either side of her snout. "You know it's true. You don't have enough energy."

She lets out a puff of steam, the sides of her rib cage collapsing inward with the release of pressure. *I know. But it kills me to think you're going without me.* She gazes at the mountains, toward the area where the dragons used to be chained. It's been converted to a base and a home for the dragons befriended by the wingless Valkyries. *You can ask one of the young ones and see if one of them wants to go with you. Although you'd probably also have to ask the Valkyrie they are bonded with. Or you could go to the dragon wastelands and ask some of the dragons you know there. Maybe even someone from my family will go with you. That would make me feel better than taking any random young and inexperienced dragon. Please tell me you're taking your friends as well and Drogon, Naga, and Tanda. I don't want you to go alone.*

"That is the plan if they are willing. Thor suggested I take my Valkyrie friends and their dragons." The edges of my mouth turn down as sadness washes over me. "I really don't want to take a different dragon, but you're not strong enough."

A shadow passes over us, and I glance up to see the underbelly of the brown dragon. Its front legs are spread wide, the membranous wings connected between the wrists and two-thirds down the torso, stretched to catch the wind as he glides through the air. Hildr's cry of excitement follows the shadow. Not long afterward, another brown dragon flies over, and I realize that Hildr, Britta, and Eir must be training the new dragon riders.

I smirk. "I guess I know where to find them."

I would feel much safer if you take them with you. They are excellent warriors, and I trust those three dragons completely.

I lean into her golden scales and slide a hand underneath the hard exterior to the soft flesh underneath. "Get better, Elan. I might not see you again before I leave, so this is my goodbye."

She nuzzles me, pushing me lightly to the side. *You're the one who needs to take care. I'll just be lying down, hanging around the Valkyrie Academy. Not my favorite place to be, by the way. To top it off, my thoughts every second of the day will be worrying about you.*

I gaze into her eyes. "I'm going to miss you."

And I you.

With a heavy heart, I leave her behind and approach the training base where I saw the four dragons and their wingless riders before. They must have been waiting for Hildr, Britta, and Eir to train them. I wait only a few minutes on the open rocky plain before Hildr passes over then circles Drogon around to land.

She climbs off Drogon and lands with a thud. Her boots crunch on the gravel as she walks toward me, running a hand through her spiky red hair to straighten it with her fingers. They momentarily catch in a small wind knot. "Hey, stranger. I was wondering when you would drop by. Have you come to help train the new dragon riders?"

I shake my head. "I wish I could, but not today. Where are Britta and Eir?"

Hildr points into the sky. In the distance, I can barely make out Naga's draconic form against the sky. His extended blue wings with the white star markings underneath are only slightly darker than the sky. I can almost make out Eir's figure sitting on the saddle on his back. Behind him is another blue dragon, practically identical to the sweet blue dragon, carrying a small speck of a Valkyrie, a new dragon rider. The two blue dragons and their riders circle over us.

"Where's Tanda?" I ask, unable to spot her yet.

"Over there." Hildr points in the opposite direction just as a red streak shoots through the sky.

The red dragon lowers and flips, and Britta clasps her saddle straps while mounted on the peak of her dragon's hump. Imitating Tanda a second later is another red dragon and a new rider on its back, whose face is ghostly white after the daring nosedive.

I chuckle. "Is there a yellow dragon? I saw a yellow dragon take off earlier as I passed through."

"It's over there." Hildr nods in another direction behind us.

Heading in our direction, close to the ground, is the yellow dragon. The dragon rider flops from side to side, face pure white with terror.

A small smile creeps onto my face. "Doesn't the rider know the dragon won't let her fall?"

Hildr harrumphs. "She hasn't learned to trust the dragon yet, and because of it, her confidence is lacking. I was hoping you would be able to help train that one. The yellow dragons are much the same as the emperor dragons, and it would be easier for her to learn from Elan and you and how the dragon moves."

I shake my head in disbelief. "I can see she needs help. We didn't get any help when we rode our dragons. It was trial and error."

"I know. But some don't learn as quickly as others."

"I can see that. I would help, but right now, I need to complete a mission for Thor. Maybe after that."

Naga circles above us before lowering and landing next to Drogon. The trainee dragon and rider land next to Hildr's trainee. In a few moments, Eir flips her leg over the blue dragon's body and slides down, hustling to greet me.

"How is Elan?" Eir suddenly squats to the ground, screaming, "Look out!"

The yellow dragon passes over our heads to land, so low that we have to duck. The new rider slides and hurtles unceremoniously off the side.

I quirk an eyebrow before pulling my attention away, returning to our conversation. "Elan's still regaining her strength. At least she's improving. Do you know if Britta is landing soon?" I search the sky for the red dragons and spot them still high in the air.

"When she sees that we've landed, she'll probably join us," Eir says. "Why do you want to know?"

"I have something to ask you three as soon as she lands."

"Let's hurry her up then." Hildr slips a forefinger and thumb into her mouth, and a high-pitched whistle pierces the silence of the sky.

Eir waves her arms, motioning Britta and Tanda to land. Moments later, Tanda takes a sudden turn and drops, followed by a confident trainee rider steering her red dragon toward the others at the last second.

After sliding to the ground, Britta straightens her black fighting leathers. "Hey, Kara. What's up?"

"I have something to ask you three," I say.

"What is it?" Eir asks.

"Thor is sending me on a mission to Jotunheim. He suggested I take you three and your dragons. But I'm not forcing you. It could be quite dangerous, and I only want you to volunteer if you want to come."

"I'm in," Hildr says about hesitation.

My jaw drops in disbelief. "You don't even know what the mission is yet."

"I'm in too," Britta says.

I shake my head. "I appreciate it. Even so, you should know what we're in for before you decide to come."

"What are we in for?" Eir's tone indicates she's coming as well.

"I need to go and see Loki's mistress. I'm going to see if we can convince her to get her children to settle down."

"Do you think it will work?" Eir asks.

Splitting my ponytail in half, I secure the band closer to my scalp. "I don't know, but we're also hoping she'll know where Loki is and tell us."

"It sounds like a long shot." Britta shrugs. "Are you taking Elan?"

I shake my head. "Elan isn't strong enough to go. I'll have to find another dragon." Suddenly, a loud thump sounds to our side. Starting, I face the noise—one hand grabbing my sword and the other clasping my necklace—ready to shoot the magic stored inside.

Chapter Six

I n the corner of my eye, I spot my friends mirroring my actions, their hands grasping their weapons and preparing their magic. My eyes sharpen on the figure before me, a golden emperor dragon slightly larger than Elan.

The dragon pulls its head back. *Dragon claws, ladies! Is that the way to greet an old friend?*

That voice is familiar. I peer at the dragon, taking in every feature. Besides being the same breed, so much about this dragon reminds me of Elan. I haven't visited the dragon wastelands in a while, but one dragon's name pops into my head.

"Sobek? Is that you?"

Of course it's me, girl. The big dragon grins, showing off too many teeth, a look that would appear more threatening to someone who wasn't a dragon rider. *Who else would I be?*

"Sorry. It's been a while since I've seen you. It's

great to see you again. What are you doing in this part of Asgard?"

I've come to see if my sister is still alive and kicking. I just flew over and spotted you guys. So here I am. I thought I'd come and say hello. He extends his wings in a grand gesture, reminding me that he had sheltered me once from the prying eyes of dragons determined to kill Valkyries. That happened just after Elan bonded with me. Things have changed so much since then.

I hadn't seen him much, other than in the last battle, protecting Asgard from a dark elf invasion. Even that was quite some time ago.

"Let me take you to Elan so you can say hello," I say.

Pfft. Sobek brushes his wings out to the sides. *I'm not that close to my sister. I know she's alive, and that's all that matters. I could see that from the sky.*

"I can feel the love." Ridicule oozes from Britta's voice.

Sobek smirks and shrugs. *Sibling love. Maybe you know how it is. It's all good, though. I can tell Mother she's fine.*

I don't remember Sobek being quite so jolly, and he seems more open and relaxed. "Then what can we do for you?"

Sobek tilts his head to the side. *You mean, what can*

I do for you? I thought I overheard that you needed a dragon to ride.

I lean on one leg, assessing him. "You *do* have good hearing. In fact, Elan recommended that I take one of her family members. Are you keen to go to Jotunheim? It could be quite dangerous."

Of course I'll go with you. Anything to protect my sister's little dragon rider. Sobek lifts his chin. *You'll be better off with me, anyway. I'm broader and bigger than Elan.*

"That would be spectacular, Sobek. Thank you." I clasp my hands in front of me, excited to find a willing and vicious dragon already. "And the cloak I made from golden emperor scales will blend in nicely with your hide."

Sobek smirks. *Probably half the scales you collected were mine.*

I chuckle. "Probably. I did collect them from the area you and your family reside."

So. When are we leaving? His scales bunch over one of his eyes as though he's lifting an eyebrow.

I gaze at my friends. "Are you fine if we leave as soon as we gather supplies? It could be a long trip. I know it was a quick trip when Loki kidnapped me, but I have a feeling this could be a bit longer. It might take some time to find her."

"That's sounds good. I don't see a problem. Do

you?" Hildr looks from Britta to Eir, who both shake their heads.

Drogon moves closer to Hildr, listening to the conversation.

"What about you, Drogon?" I ask.

I want to stop these beasts. I don't want the same thing happening to the other dragons as what Elan went through. I'm willing to try the peaceful approach. Drogon's dark-brown eyes are serious. *I don't speak for the other dragons, though.*

Naga slips next to Eir. *Naga goes anywhere Eir goes.*

"Of course I'm going." Eir cuddles into Naga's neck, and Naga wraps himself around the peaceful Valkyrie.

Tanda joins us, standing next to Britta.

"How about you, Tanda?" I ask. "You have a say as well."

Tanda's bright-red eyes focus on me. Before she became a friend, they were quite terrifying. She nods. *I will not let Britta down. I will go with her to help and to protect her.*

After explaining to the student dragon riders that we could be away for a few days, we travel to our rooms with the dragons following. Because we got along so well, we decided to live together. The accommodation is similar to the dormitory we shared at the academy, but we have separate bedrooms and a living room. A couple of soft blue leather double lounge chairs section the open room off from the dining area consisting of a small round dining table and four seats.

I grab my pack and my saddle, hoping it will fit around Sobek's broad body. Carrying my cloak, I sling my sword, bow, and quiver of arrows onto my back. Then I grab another bag and fill it with water and whatever food would travel well, most of which I've stashed from my trips to the palace. Thankfully, I grabbed enough snacks for a few days. Dragging the large saddle along the floor and out the door is a struggle. A strange look passes over Sobek's face momentarily but washes away before I can ask.

He squats down to the ground as though he's a natural at having a rider on his back. As he hunkers down, I toss the top of the saddle over his back, flinging the straps over the other side. The buckle of the main belt barely reaches the other end, making it a mission to connect them across his chest. I secure additional straps under his wings, where they join his body, and hook some at the connection where his legs join his body. I make sure each additional scale I'd attached to the leads faces out, ready to turn invisible with Sobek if the situation requires. I toss the reins over the top of his head and clasp it with one hand, the other hand grasping the saddle as I pull myself up.

Something suddenly occurs to me. "Sobek. Have you had a rider on your back before?"

His voice seems amused. *No. I haven't.*

Suddenly my stomach twists into knots. "Do you think you're going to handle it?"

Of course I will, he scoffs.

"Perhaps you should fly a quick round first," I suggest. "Let's jump to the sky and do a couple of circles overhead. That way, we can get a feel for each other and create some understanding so you know exactly what I want when I ask for it."

Sure thing. Without warning, he pushes off into the sky, and my stomach lurches. I didn't have time to prepare my body for the sudden jerk, and his spring from the ground was faster than Elan's. After the escalation stops, we tilt to one side a little. My backside skids that way, and I clasp firmly onto the reins, trying to prevent myself from sliding off.

"A little warning would be nice next time."

Oh? I thought you would be used to it. Sobek's wings rise and fall in a steady motion, taking us several yards higher. Suddenly he nosedives and twists to one side, his body gliding sideways, and I struggle again to stay on. I squeeze my legs into the saddle as close to his body as I can. My knuckles turn white as

I grip the straps. He straightens, and when I gain control, my clamped jaw relaxes. "Can you give me a bit of warning before you do that?"

You need warning even over that? Surprise sounds in Sobek's voice. The golden dragon straightens and flies higher, continuing his climb for a few minutes and gaining a lot of height. Suddenly, he flips upside down and furls his wings by his sides. The feeling of falling shoots bile to my stomach, and I long to throw up. I drop from the saddle, my knuckles ache from clasping, and my feet slip out of the stirrups. My whole body flips and dangles, the ground calling me to a harsh death below, leaving me hanging with my feet below, the wrong way from the saddle. My only savior is my white-knuckled grip on the reins hanging around his neck.

Chapter Seven

"Sobek!" I scream.

He flips back over. My stomach lurches to my feet from the force, and as he rights himself, I'm flung to his other side, slamming against his flank. My arms sear with pain, and my hands burn from clasping the straps. Drawing from my core, I launch one leg over his back and pull while using my leg as a lever, flipping myself to the top and finally sitting upright.

His body shakes underneath me, accompanied by a strange sound. It almost sounds like a chuckle.

"Sobek. Did you do that on purpose?"

Of course. His chuckle broadens, reverberating in my head. *I have to keep you on your toes and see what you can handle.*

I tap his scales playfully. "Stop it!"

What's the problem? Don't worry. If you fall, I'll catch you.

"And why do I not feel comforted?"

Just trying to make sure you're paying attention. I'd hate for you to go into the land of the frost giants and forget to concentrate. I think my sister has been too soft on you.

"Hmm." I push my lips to one side. "I think I'll be fine without your antics, thank you. I'm starting to think cheekiness runs in your family."

I don't know what you mean. Mother is ever so serious.

"Yes, she lacks the mischief that you two have. After all, she is the leader of the dragons. You would think some of her sensibility would rub off on her children."

He smirks over his shoulder. *Now, where's the fun in that?*

We fly a few more rounds of the area, these trips much smoother than the first, leaving me with no trouble staying on. Sobek lands next to my friends and their dragons. Wasting no time, I climb off his back and sit on the solid ground. Never have I been so glad to sit on hard earth.

Eir sits next to me on a large rock. "It looks like you had quite a rough ride. It looked kind of scary, actually."

"Yes. Apparently, Sobek was just keeping me on my toes, trying to make sure I won't get distracted on our mission." I shake a fist at him, and he chuckles, showing off his broad array of dangerous teeth.

I dust off my clothes, pulling at the hems to straighten them as though this would calm myself after such a rough ride. When I stop fiddling with my clothes, my breath returns, bringing a small amount of peace, clearing my mind, and enabling me to think. I frown. "I just had a thought. I haven't taken a dragon anywhere but Midgard. Does anyone know the best way for dragons to travel to the other realms? The Bifrost is out. It only travels to Midgard."

Blank faces stare back at me, and I'm at a loss. I can't think of anyone who knows how to get them there. I'm starting to believe we have failed before we begin when Sobek's voice enters my head.

We can go through Yggdrasil. When I look at him, confused, he shrugs. *I thought it was common knowledge.*

Astonished, I gaze at him. "The branches are big enough for humans and some smaller giants, but not for dragons."

"Then how did that lava monster get in?" Britta asks.

I push my tongue against my teeth and frown. "That's the thing. I don't know."

Sobek slowly paces my way, his long golden legs regal. *It is true that most of the World Tree only allows smaller creatures and beings through, and it isn't big enough for dragons of my size. But the main trunk of Yggdrasil is vast and can carry several dragons in a row.*

That finally makes sense. "So that's how Loki got all those dragons back to Asgard when he attacked."

Sadness flashes through Sobek's eyes but disappears quickly. Perhaps he remembered the day they had to fight against their own kind. *Yes. That would be how he got all those dragons into Asgard at the same time.*

"Do you know where it is?" Eir asks Sobek.

I don't understand. I thought it was common knowledge. The scales above Sobek's eyes crumple together in a frown.

Not to us, it's not, Drogon says.

Oh. Sobek looks puzzled.

"Can you show us the way, Sobek?" I ask.

Sure. Just climb onto my back, and let's go. He stoops down again, and I climb back on, securing my feet in the stirrups and fasten the extra strap around my ankles before hanging on tightly to the reins. I glower at the back of his head. "No funny games, Sobek."

I'll see what I can do. The cheek remains in his voice.

The flight across Asgard to Yggdrasil's main trunk, where it was large enough for the dragons, wasn't as quick as I hoped. We pass several of the small branches of the World Tree, where Ratatoskr had peered through holes and rested on smaller branches.

Sobek leads us to the middle of Asgard. The bright sun burns against our skin, acting like a wall of heat pushing us away, making us labor to the end.

After a few hours of flight, Sobek glides gracefully to the ground, landing at the base of an enormous trunk growing almost at the center of Asgard.

The trunk's width is impressive, and I don't doubt it will allow the passage of several dragons.

Thankfully, the trip is graceful and steady, absent Sobek's antics. As I climb off his back, a flash of red scurries along the bark of the World Tree, grabbing my attention. It almost looks like the colors of Ratatoskr. By the time I can focus on the area, no red is to be found, and furry, snarky critters are definitely absent from Yggdrasil's branches. However, I wouldn't be surprised if the little squirrel is up to something.

Thumps of the other dragons landing sound behind us seconds after we land, and Eir and Hildr dismount their dragons.

"What a lovely, huge tree." Eir shamelessly approaches the massive trunk and wraps her arms around it as far as they can go. She pulls back and runs her fingers over the bark, her hand jerking from the roughness of the dips, and rises. Her face is passionate and peaceful, filled with love as she gazes up into its branches dreamily. "I wish we had more trees on Asgard like there are in Midgard. It would be much more beautiful."

"Agreed." Britta climbs off Tanda, struggling slightly with the height that Tanda's hump creates, compared to the other dragons. With her feet firmly on the ground, she tucks some loose strands of brown hair behind her ear and circles around the broad trunk of the World Tree. She pauses and calls back, "Is this the entrance?"

Sobek wanders over to her, and all the riders and dragons follow. We gaze at a deep hole in the trunk, big enough to allow a dragon the size of Sobek, if not bigger.

Sobek sticks his head into the hole, his voice echoing through the void. *That's the one.*

"Jeez. It's no wonder the big lava monster got through. This hole is huge." Eir hangs on to the side of the gap, peering over the edge.

Hildr screws up her nose. "Still, the lava monster would have a challenge to fit through the hole, although it wouldn't be impossible."

I gaze into the hole. Light is pushed away by darkness, giving the impression that it dominates the whole way through. "It's hard to tell exactly how big it is, although the void is rather impressive." I observe Sobek, assessing his size and the expanse of his wings. Fitting through would be tight for him, but he talks as though he's done it before. Turning my gaze upward inside the trunk, I'm met by darkness again and maybe a hint of light in the distance. Seeing is going to be impossible. I'm glad we have dragons. They can see much better than us in the dark.

Turning to the other dragons and my friends, I say, "Well, this is it. It's the last chance to pull out before we leave Asgard."

As if muttered at once, I'm met with a jumble of similar words. "Not likely to happen."

I tighten the straps of my bag over my shoulders and secure my quiver, bow, and sword firmly in place on my back. Then I close a flap over my quiver to keep the arrows from falling out before turning to the others. "Let's do this."

Chapter Eight

S tanding at the edge of the hole in the World Tree, I creep a little farther over the edge for a final look into the dark abyss, searching for some sign of light or a hole that would act as an exit into another realm. With the exit remaining hidden, I grasp a small lip inside the trunk and peer over the edge a little farther. My feet slip, and suddenly, I'm hurtling over the edge and into the darkness of the abyss, my hands grasping for anything, struggling to find purchase. I dangle over the edge, barely grabbing hold of the inside of the trunk. Fear pulls the strength from my fingers and weakens my arms, right when I need the energy the most. Still weak from Sobek's earlier antics, my fingers slip. I squeal and grit my teeth, tightening my grasp and mustering enough strength to pull myself up.

Something grabs my arms and wrists, securing

them firmly. I look up to find Hildr and Britta hunkering down and dragging me up the rough surface to the ground.

"Oh, Vanir!" Hildr exclaims. "What are you trying to do, fall to your death?"

Using their strength, I scramble to the ground and lie flat, panting. "I was trying to find the next exit out of the tree. I can't see any above or below." My chest heaves, and I lie still for a few minutes, thankful for the solid surface under me. My racing heart takes a while to settle. "Does anyone know their way through the World Tree to Jotunheim?"

I do, of course. Sobek plunks his backside next to me. *If you asked me, I could have told you and saved you some excitement.*

Heaving myself up, I assess him with a furrowed brow. "Have you been there before?"

He flicks his golden wings before furling them against his golden body. His gaze drops to the ground for an instant then back up, a conniving smirk on his face. *I may have traveled down there to have a look around—you know, to see what they were doing with the young dragons stolen from our herd. I needed to find out how the dragons were being treated and their living conditions before they returned home.*

I plant my hands on my hips. "Huh. I had no idea Eingana sent anybody down to have a look."

Sobek's gaze is sheepish. *That's because she didn't send me. I had a look on my own.* He presses his chest against the ground and lifts a scaly eyebrow at me. *Are you going to climb on, or what?*

I duck underneath his extended golden wing and climb onto the saddle, hooking my feet in the stirrups and clasping the reins.

Okay, Valkyries and dragons, it's time to go. Sobek stands and charges into the hole, diving off the edge with his wings tucked down at his sides. My stomach rises to my throat, as though I left it in Asgard, as the freefall takes over my body and we careen endlessly down.

The pressure of the wind forces my cheeks up toward the hole we exited. After a moment, I gather the strength to spin my head to look behind us and see if the others have followed us through the hole. Far in the distance, small specks are blocking the tiny ray of light from our exit. Then my hair whips over my face, blocking my vision, and I flick my head around to face the front, which pushes the long strands behind me again. A chill bites into my fighting leathers, and I clasp my numb fingers tighter around the reins. I never know when Sobek will decide to test my riding skills again. Even though Sobek protected me in the dragon wastelands when Elan left me in his care, he isn't Elan, and riding a different dragon feels strange.

The fall continues beyond an extended, comfortable timeframe. I thought this direct route would be quicker than the way the abducting frost giant took me. Surely, climbing down individual branches of a tree would take longer than a freefall. Then again, perhaps I was paranoid.

The strange feeling takes over my stomach, and I close my eyes to wish the sensation away, only to find that makes it worse. I pry my eyes open, glancing into the darkness, disappointed when we pass a patch of light without stopping.

"What was that?" I ask.

It was just one of the exits. The indifference in Sobek's voice annoys me. *It's not the one we want.*

"How can you be sure?" I ask. "We didn't even get to look inside."

"Because I've been here before," Sobek says. "There are many more of those to pass before we get to Jotunheim."

We continue freefalling, and a bug flies into my mouth. I clamp my jaw shut and attempt to spit it out. A few more patches of light flash by, then suddenly, Sobek extends his wings, and we flip and reel straight into the light. My brain slaps against my skull, giving me a headache, the feeling intensifying when Sobek slams his feet down. We skip across the ground, Sobek's tail bumping behind us, and his wings extend to capture the wind like a parachute.

I want to thump him for the lack of warning. When we finally come to a halt, my wind-whipped hair swings around my face, getting caught in the wet trails from my nose and mouth. My body rocks back in the saddle, and my hands are frozen from the cold and lack of movement as I'm too scared to release my grip on the reins. After a few moments, my nerves settle as my eyes focus on snow-tipped mountaintops surrounded by a frozen river. The river snakes through the deep valley crusted in ice, and I'm confident we've arrived in the land of the frost giants.

Three soft thuds sound behind me, the landings entirely different from the one I just endured. When I turn, I'm greeted by the peaceful faces of my friends, who appear to have been on a carefree flight.

"That was a fast fall, Sobek." Eir shoots him a curious look as she casually climbs off Naga.

Kara wanted to get here in a hurry. So I did as she wanted. I live only to serve. Sobek folds a wing across his chest and bows, his golden eyes mocking me over his shoulder as he bends his front legs.

I slide down off his back, my feet landing on the hard, icy ground with a crunch. After a few steps, I work out the wobble in my walk, my nerves refusing to settle. I stumble over my feet, and Eir catches my arm, preventing my fall.

"Thanks," I breathe to Eir.

"No problem." Her eyes peer toward the horizon as she searches the icy tips of this land, which appears absent of all life. "Are we in the right place?"

"Yes. It looks how I remember it." I rub the chill from my arms.

The cracking of ice behind me announces Britta's approach. "Which way do we go now?"

"I don't know. Last time I was here, the frost giant dragged me to the tunnel straightaway and placed me in a cave. There was no time for sightseeing, and Loki only had me here for a little while." I face Sobek, surprised to see peace and contentment on his face, almost as though he loves it here. "Do you know where to go, Sobek?"

Sobek lowers his nose down to my level. *No. But I'm happy to look around.*

"It looks like that is the only option we have," Britta says.

Hildr joins us, standing by Eir and observing the mountain peaks. Hot dragon breath warms our backs as they gaze over our heads.

"What do we have here?" a strange voice says behind us. "Did you hear me calling for you, my snacks?"

Standing behind the dragons is an enormous blue-skinned frost giant.

Chapter Nine

The big blue giant towers over us. "Hmm. Scrawny. Not much of a snack." He rubs his beard, a contemplative expression on his face.

Broad shoulders, approximately six times the width of Thor's, slope away from his head. Thick arms, about twice the thickness of an Einherjar, frame either side of his thick torso. The blue-skinned giant's legs seem tiny underneath the vast body, yet they're still several times the average man's height.

Disbelief plagues me—just our luck to be discovered the second we arrive in Jotunheim. I forgot how lucky I was the last time I was escorted in frost giant country by Loki. His shape-shifting form alone guaranteed safe passage through this land.

If I was sitting on Sobek's back, it would raise my position to about the height of the giant's groin. I forgot how big these giants could be. After all, some time has passed since we fought the frost giants in

Asgard. This specimen would tower over the dwarf giants Loki used for his army. Compared to this frost giant, the dwarf giants were more like large humans. This giant is so big that it's ridiculous. I hope this guy is friendly, but something deep inside is crushing all that hope. Frost giants are renowned for disliking Valkyries, and he's looking at us like we're food.

The giant's voice booms down at us. "You look like battle maidens, but you don't have wings." He rubs the bald patch on top of his head, circled by a loop of golden-blond hair falling in straight strands past his shoulders.

Cupping my hands around my mouth, I yell up to the giant, "Yes, we are! But we come in peace! We're not here to fight like the winged Valkyries would be!"

A loud rumble exits the giant's mouth in a husky laugh, and his belly wobbles as he holds it. "Do you think I'm worried about four little women?" He tugs at the end of his long mustache and wipes the corner of an eye.

Climbing onto Sobek's back, I stare up at him in disbelief. He's laughing at us. Anger warms my insides as I assess the other three Valkyries. Hildr's face burns red at the insult, and her hand twitches over her sword hilt.

I need two large breaths to calm my anger. When I think I can project a calm voice, I call up to the giant, trying a slightly different tactic. "We're not here to cause trouble. We're here to look for Loki's mistress, Angrboda."

The giant's laughing subsides for a moment as he bends over to peer down at me. He rubs the base of his beard, braided against his chest. "Is that so?" Stale breath blows over my face.

A cough stems from a strangled gasp, and I splutter away, turning my head momentarily. After regaining composure, I gaze directly into the giant's eyes as he remains bent over gawking at me. "Yes, that is so."

"Then let me take you to her." The giant swipes his hand at Sobek and me, his fingers constricting as he attempts to grab us.

"Move, Sobek!" I yell.

The golden dragon jumps to the side, narrowly dodging the giant's hand, and pushes up, flapping his wings, attempting to take to the sky. The giants swipes a hand left, then right, narrowly missing Sobek. Groaning with frustration, the giant aims a little higher, attempting to clasp Sobek's feet or body. The dragon's movements are jagged, knocking my position in the saddle, and I struggle to maintain my hold on Sobek's reins and stay on his back. The attempt uses all my concentration.

As the swipes grow closer, I shriek, "Keep dodging, Sobek! Zigzag up into the sky."

Sobek follows my orders, and the bumpy, awkward ride continues. I gaze over my shoulder and see the three other dragons are doing the same. The giant continues swiping at Sobek and me, his giant hand swiping every direction. Finally, Sobek manages to fly out of the giant's reach. After missing his opportunity with Sobek, the giant suddenly swipes lower, trying his luck with the others.

"Stop!" I scream when he narrowly misses Drogon and Hildr.

With a questioning gaze, the giant peers at me.

"You don't need to grasp us to show us where Angrboda is."

Disbelief covers the giant's face. "Where's the fun in that? I've always wanted to hold a dragon."

His hands work at Drogon. The dragon spreads his wings and dives, gliding rapidly toward the ground before suddenly swerving up, the maneuver taking advantage of his batlike wings.

With a face blanched whiter than a ghost, Hildr glances over her shoulder. When she realizes she is out of the giant's reach, the color returns to her cheeks. Seconds later, a rumble rises from the ground, and a scream rings out. The giant breaks into a jog, his face beaming with excitement and arms flying, like a child chasing a butterfly. I watch in horror as the giant takes another swipe at my friends, the ground rumbling its protest with each monstrous step. Each step is several wing paces for a dragon as our scaly friends attempt to fly up and away.

Tanda's slower form struggles more than the others to get out of the giant's reach. The stocky blue hands swipe at the red dragon and Britta, and my friends barely manage to swerve away.

Reaching over my shoulder, I retrieve my bow and nock an arrow from the quiver to shoot at the giant's hand. The arrow digs into one of his finger-tips, looking as big as a pin in a human hand. The giant pauses midswipe, opens his hand, palm up, and stares at the arrow sticking out of his finger pad.

Confusion washes over the blue face, and after a brief pause, his voice booms, "But you said you come in peace." His mouth drops open as he stares at me, his eyes filled with hurt.

I square my shoulders as Sobek remains out of the giant's reach. "We do come in peace, but we do not come as your playthings." The distraction gives my friends time to rise beyond clasping distance. "You can show us where to find Loki's mistress without handling us."

Sadness swamps the giant's face. "You don't want to be handled by giants?"

Hildr screws up her face in disapproval, pushing her freckles together. "You got that right."

"But you're so cute, and your dragons are adorable. I want to hold one in my hand." The giant opens a hand as though imagining a dragon resting on his palm.

I shake my head. "I'm afraid that's not going to happen without permission."

"It's definitely not!" Britta yells over Tanda's side.

"So how can I show you the way?" the giant asks, looking lost and confused.

"You can walk that way, and we will follow," Eir calls as Naga lowers and hovers in front of the giant.

When I see her position, my heart thumps against my rib cage. She's too close. I swear she's too close. The sweet, ever-trusting Eir believes that things will listen to us and our words and do as we ask. Sometimes her peaceful mind can get us into a lot of danger.

My jaw tenses as I call between clenched teeth, "Eir. Join us up here."

She peers up at me with a smile. "He's listening to us."

"Please, Eir." Panic strains Hildr's voice. "Come join us up here."

Eir sighs audibly, sounding disappointed. "Okay." She pulls on Naga's reins, directing him to turn. His big blue eyes land on me, filled with compassion, almost a reflection of Eir's most used expression. They are a good match for peace, but not for situations like this.

Something moves behind them, and a large blue hand flings in their way. "Awww. I like blue dragons. It's my favorite color." The giant's hand continues to swipe.

"Look out, Eir!" Britta screeches as she whips out her bow and nocks an arrow. "Oh, no, you don't. Not on my watch," she mutters into her poised hand, releasing the arrow straight into the giant's hand. This time, the giant doesn't stop. Instead, the hand moves closer and closer to Eir and Naga. The size of it would swallow them up within the confines of the hand. Britta releases another arrow. The aim is true but, at the last second, narrowly misses the giant's hand, failing to stop the swipe accelerating toward Naga and Eir as it moves in a slightly different direction.

Chapter Ten

"Noooo!" Britta screams the word, dragging it out into a howl.

Jumping, I toss the bow into my left hand and reach for my sword with my right. Sliding metal scrapes as I retrieve my sword from its sheath on my back. When I feel the sword's freedom, I twist the angle and fling it straight at the giant's hand, swiping for Naga and Eir. The sword glides and straightens as though tossed like a dagger, my magic steering it straight toward the giant's wrist. Hope rises in my heart as the aim flies true.

The giant grunts, a displeased expression filling his face as the point of the sword digs deep into his skin, yet his hand doesn't stop. His fingers wrap around Eir and Naga.

Grasping Naga's legs between index finger and thumb, the giant holds him in front of his face, with

Eir clasping onto Naga's reins. "I like dragons." The giant pulls my two friends closer to his face, Eir's knuckles white from the strain of holding on. "And this one is just an itty-bitty one. It's cute." He twists Naga's body in different directions, displaying Naga's terrified face and circled mouth. "Look at those big blue eyes." The blue monster chuckles, hitching up his long brown pants, which slipped down his backside while he jogged.

Hildr cups her mouth. "Douse him with fire, Naga!"

Naga's eyes widen as he stares from the giant to Hildr, looking stunned.

Using his spare hand, the giant plucks the sword out of his skin and tosses it over his shoulder then clasps Naga tightly in his hand as Naga peers through the gaps of the fingers. Even if Naga wanted to shoot fire, his lungs are probably squashed and unable to suck in enough oxygen.

Using my magic, I call to my sword, the wings on the hilt growing and flapping their way toward me. Blood spills down the giant's arm, and momentarily the giant looks put out. Then he shrugs.

His big blond brows furrow as he peers at us. "Seeing you battle maidens aren't going to play nice, I'm going to take this little blue dragon and its rider and go play with them. They seem like the nice ones." He closes his entire hand around Naga and Eir, hiding them from view. The giant's jaw rises. "And I'm not going to give them back."

For a moment, I stare at the giant's back in disbelief as he marches in the opposite direction. I study the size and shape of the giant and the long leather pants he wears under his potbelly. I'm dumbstruck that he's simply grabbed another living being—two, in fact—and carried them away. Ice shatters as the large footsteps pound their way through the valley.

As I sit in a daze, a distant voice hails me. *Kara. Calling Kara.* The words bounce against the soft walls of my brain, only vaguely registering. *Kara. Calling Kara. Hello-o-o, Kara. Come in, Kara.* Suddenly my seat drops away from underneath me.

My mouth drops open as I'm jolted out of my stupor. The reins rip across the skin of my hand, and I instantly feel the burn. Wind gushes up from underneath me, blowing my hair to the sky. I'm falling.

I glance down at the dragon beneath me and scream, "What are you doing, Sobek?"

His wings push out horizontally, catching the wind and halting our fall. *You're welcome.*

I growl at the smug tone in his voice.

He chuckles. *I was shaking you out of your trance.*

That giant is taking off with your friends, and you're doing nothing about it.

I shake my head, trying to clear it. "You're right."

Silver glints in the light and catches my eye. I clasp the hilt of my sword after realizing it followed me in the dive. As soon as my hand wraps around it, the extended wings retract back into their metal shape, and I slide it back into its sheath. Wrapping both hands around the reins, I sit forward in the saddle. "Let's go, Sobek. After that giant!"

Sobek accelerates, flapping as fast as he can. Drogon and Hildr join us on the left-hand side and Tanda carrying Britta on the right, their smaller frames struggling to keep up with the emperor dragon. As I grip the reins more tightly, my nails dig into my palms, and I will Sobek to fly faster. The distance between us and the giant is increasing. Disappointment grows within me with each enormous step the giant takes. Sobek's wings flap faster, yet the gap extends in moments. To make things worse, fresh snow is falling, covering the tracks of the giant.

"Fly faster, Sobek!" My high-pitched scream grates in my own eardrums. Still, the distance grows.

Panting sounds in my head, followed by a voice filled with disapproval. *What do you think I'm doing?*

I groan in frustration. I wish I had enough magic

and knowledge to encase the giant in a stunning spell. Instead, I'm cursed to watch the gap between my friends and us extend. I can't lose Eir like this again, plus Naga too. I know Sobek is flying as quickly as he can, but I still can't help saying, "I swear Elan flies faster than this, and she's smaller than you."

A low growl radiates through my head, deeper than Elan's ever could. I've insulted Sobek, and I don't care. All that I want is my friends back.

Tanda's red form slowly disappears behind us, her strangely irregular shape struggling to keep up with the speed of the emperor dragon. On the other side, Drogon pumps his wings faster, his body bigger and leaner, making his progress better than Tanda's, yet he still struggles to keep up with Sobek.

Sobek pushes himself harder, attempting to close the gap to the massive blue giant. Drogon's movement disappears from my peripheral vision, and I turn to locate my friends. Their progress has slowed dramatically, their bodies unable to keep up with the larger form of the emperor dragon.

"It's just you and me now, Sobek." I return my gaze to the front, and my eyes widen. The frost giant has disappeared.

"Where did he go?" My heart beats rapidly with panic.

Don't worry. I'm on it. Sobek pants, pushing his wings even faster. *Don't you have a cloak?*

"Why do you ask? I'm not cold." My blood is pumping so hard that my body hasn't had a chance to get cold, even surrounded by snow-capped mountains.

Seriously. That's your answer?

Dumbfounded, I sit still for a moment before I realize what he means. He's talking about the dragon-scale cloak. "Of course." I curse my own stupidity. Unlatching the flap of my saddle pouch, I pry it open over the saddle, pull out the cloak, and slide my arms through the sleeves before raising the hood over my head.

Sobek disappears underneath me, giving the impression that I'm flying on my own. For a moment, it rattles my nerves. It's a sensation that I've felt many times with Elan, but she's a familiar dragon that has my complete trust. I squeeze my fingers tightly around the reins, square my shoulders, and shake off my nerves. I'm being ridiculous. This is Elan's brother. He's trustworthy, even if he tried to prank me initially. He's protected me in the past.

Suddenly we flip, and my body flies horizontally as we round the corner of a mountain. Large frosty clumps stick out of a mountain near my head, and I have to duck to avoid the collision. Small waterfalls run down the mountainside, developed from melting snow. Sobek unexpectantly flips again to an upright position, and my body slides in the saddle. The wind from his wings brushes against my leather pants, reminding me of the effort he's exerting to speed forward.

Squinting, I catch sight of the frost giant's back in the distance, barely visible through the falling snow. At least Elan's brother has managed to keep up with him so far.

"Good job, Sobek." The words shoot from my mouth before I consider that this probably sounds condescending. "What I mean is keep up what you're doing." I try to correct myself but end up sounding like a schoolteacher talking to a young student.

Sobek's wings pump harder underneath me, and the cold from the snow bites into my skin. Even though Sobek has managed to keep track of the giant so far, the distance is growing between us, and the fear of losing my friends twists massive knots in my stomach. Worry is starting to wear at me, the fear escalating when the frost giant rapidly turns and runs behind a mountain.

"Hurry, Sobek!"

I'm sure Sobek is cursing me under his breath. Even so, his wings pump harder. The distance to that mountain tears at my nerves. Suddenly, Sobek flips to glide around the corner, lurching my body sideways and leaving me flying horizontally again. After a moment, he straightens then halts, and we are confronted with an empty plain. The frost giant, Naga, and Eir are nowhere to be found.

Chapter Eleven

Sobek circles the plain, covering its boundary with the snow-capped mountains. Every gap is scrutinized as we check for an enormous blue figure. It's hard to believe that something so massive could disappear like this. But this frost giant has indeed managed to vanish, taking my friends with him. With our invisibility hiding us, he doesn't even know Sobek and I have followed him. After the first round proves unsuccessful, Sobek tries again. He hovers at the entrance to each channel between the mountains, searching for any sign of life.

My heart aches. "Where did they go, Sobek?"

I don't know. So much regret rings in those words. *I'll circle around again just in case he's hiding in a nook somewhere.* Remaining invisible, we check again, this time slower than the last two, making sure our haste hasn't caused us to miss something vital.

Each empty valley we observe causes my heart to fall further into my stomach.

We're back where we started, hovering at the spot, when a scream grabs our attention.

My eyes widen. "What was that?"

I don't know. Let's check it out.

We fly back the way we came, our eyes peeled, searching for Hildr, Drogon, Tanda, and Britta. Snow falls rapidly, obscuring our vision past a few yards. The lack of clear vision accentuates the tension running through my limbs. The empty countryside is eerie in the wake of danger. Sobek veers to the right, back onto the original path, and we almost collide with Drogon. My spirits rise when I spot Hildr on his back, my hands straining with the effort to hang on as Sobek struggles to dodge them and right ourselves.

"Stop, Sobek!" I screech.

Sobek circles back and hovers by Drogon's side. I yank my hood off my head, exposing myself to Hildr. She jerks with a start, her face pale and her eyes wide until she realizes it's us.

"What was that?" I ask.

"I don't know. I think it might have been Britta. I can't find her and Tanda anywhere. They must've been snapped up by another giant. You would think a red dragon is easy to spo—"

I slap a palm on my forehead as dread fills my stomach. "Of course. A red dragon in a frosty blue atmosphere will be easy to spot. How could I be so stupid? I should have told them not to come."

"It's not your fault," Hildr says. "Besides, I'm sure they would have come anyway."

"But I could have insisted that they stay behind. I'm the one that has been here before. I should have remembered the realm is a dull blue and filled with ice. It's suitable for the frost giants and not a place you take a red dragon if you don't want to be found."

"That may be so, but we're on a search mission for Loki's mistress. We hadn't intended to be hunted by the frost giants."

In frustration, I slap my thigh. "Then we're stupid. We're four Valkyries, for goodness' sake. We're trained to fight. We should have been smarter about it."

"And I'm telling you Britta wouldn't have stayed behind anyway. We'll find them. We've just got to keep looking." Hildr searches in the direction we just came from. "Did you find Naga and Eir?"

I shake my head. "We had run out of options and wondered which way to go next when we heard the scream."

Drogon suddenly spins and heads in the opposite direction.

Hildr clasps her reins more tightly. "What is it, Drogon?"

I can smell Tanda.

"You can smell Tanda?" Hildr frowns.

Of course. I can smell dragons. Haven't I told you that?

Sobek and I follow as they pursue Tanda's scent.

Hildr's voice trails back to me. "No. You haven't told me that."

Drogon looks over his shoulder, his pointed horns poking out in every direction from his head and neck. *I guess I didn't think it was necessary before. But the brown dragons have a heightened sense of smell, especially when it comes to other dragons.*

"That's good to know. And what a time to bring it up," Hildr says.

The falling snow tapers off into a light dust, clearing a longer visual distance. Sobek increases his speed, lining us up with Hildr and Drogon.

"What do you know about frost giants?" I ask.

Drogon peers sideways at me. *Who are you asking?*

I shrug. "Everyone."

Hildr shakes her head. "Not much. Other than they're considered enemies of Asgard."

"What about you, Drogon?" I ask.

They aren't my favorite beings, Drogon grumbles.

"Sobek?"

Some of them are known to be nasty.

"No kidding!" I say. "I think we've worked that out."

But there are a few pleasant ones, Sobek adds as a last-minute thought.

"Only a few?" Hildr tilts her head.

Yeah. Just a few.

"You aren't making me feel better, Sobek." I tap his scales near the saddle.

Oh? I didn't realize that was my job. A displeased snort travels through his mind projection. *I thought my job was to give you an honest answer about what I know about them.*

Expelled air whistles through my teeth. "You're right. Although I was hoping for some good news."

We follow Drogon around a few more corners until we eventually spot the back of a frost giant in the distance. This giant is lean, unlike the giant that captured Eir and Naga. His torso is bare, his ribs slightly visible through his blue skin. The giant rubs his bald head, and his stance almost seems uncertain.

"Did that giant come from our way, Drogon?" Hildr asks.

Drogon lifts his nose, and his nostrils cave slightly as he sucks in a deep breath. *I think it did. The scent leads me that way.*

We pursue the frost giant, Drogon's nostrils twitching in the wind. The frost giant presses forward, slow and steady, then pauses, gazes downward, and hunches over something in its hand. The distance between us closes as the frost giant is unaware of us closing in on him.

My hope rises slightly, but at the same time, I'm apprehensive about what we're about to face. I embrace my inner warrior, ready for whatever may come.

When we near, I pull the hood of my scale cape over my head. In our invisible form, Sobek and I circle around the giant's front, catching a glimpse of what's in his hand.

My neck stiffens, and before I can stop myself, I mutter, "It's Tanda and Britta."

The giant turns, searching for my voice.

Good one, bright spark, Sobek retorts. *He heard you.* Sobek backs away from the giant, giving us some distance from any swinging limbs.

The giant continues to search, confusion growing on his face. Several lines are etched in grooves in his face, giving him a freakish appearance.

Tanda's red legs and head poke out from the hand, her red body framed by his fingers, which are spread to grasp the dragon. It's hard to believe that something as significant as a dragon can look so small in comparison. The giant pinches Tanda's legs between his forefinger and thumb and opens his hand farther, exposing Britta sitting on her back, the Valkyrie's jaw set in determination.

Despite her predicament, Tanda continues to fight for herself and her rider. She flaps her wings, hovering in place, her secured leg stopping her from traveling. A plume of fire expels from her nose at the giant's face. Swiftly, the giant pulls back, tuts, then clasps his hand around the dragon. Terror flares in her red eyes, dulling with hope when she spots Drogon and Hildr hovering behind the giant.

"You're a pretty red dragon. You're so cute," the giant says. "But what do I do with you? And why are you flying in our lands? Perhaps I'll be able to eat you."

"Oh no, you're not." Britta shakes her fist at the giant. "Not on my watch."

The giant snorts with amusement, and the gust of wind pushes over Britta's face, flicking her brown hair behind her shoulders.

Nothing is holding Britta in Tanda's saddle. She can leave her dragon as soon as she has an opportunity, yet she remains on Tanda's saddle, firmly clasping the reins. Flicking her palm at the giant, Britta releases a pulse of magic at the giant's face, landing it on his nose.

Sweat gathers on my forehead in anticipation. Ever since we lost our magic trainer, Gilroma, our magic has improved very little. Britta has had less training than me, and after pumping all my magic energy into Elan and seeing very few results, I fear Britta's magic would do nothing to the giant. If anything, it would probably annoy him.

The giant's nose bunches into a strange shape, then his head flings back then forward in a rapid motion as he sneezes all over Britta and Tanda, covering them in snot.

Ewww! That's just wrong! Disgust fills Sobek's voice.

Screwing up her face, Britta wipes the gooey mess out of her eyes and off her face, curling her lip. Tanda flaps her wings, taking advantage of a slightly loosened grip, and the goop flings off them, her fiery eyes glaring at the giant.

As I suspected, Britta's magic wasn't enough to hurt the giant. However, it did give me an idea. I need to get a message to the others somehow, but we can't yell to communicate. That would alert the giant to our next move. Even if Sobek and I flew to their side in our invisible form to speak to them, the giant would probably hear us.

Pulling on Sobek's reins, I direct him away from

the giant, hopefully out of earshot. "Sobek. How far can your mind speak travel?"

Fairly far. Why?

"Can you talk to the others from here?"

He scoffs. *Well, yeah. They're not that far. Hasn't Elan told you how far she can speak?*

"It's not exactly something I've needed to ask her before. Although I do remember her talking to me through the academy walls even though we couldn't see each other." I growl. "Anyway, we need to coordinate our magic attacks."

But you just saw how that went for Britta. If you want to be covered in snot, you're on your own.

I cluck my tongue. "That's not what I was aiming for, and you know it. I can't believe you're making jokes at a time like this. Elan likes her jokes, but she still knows when it's time to be serious." I dig a boot into his side.

There's no need to get nasty. Sobek growls. *I can't believe you're going to stoop so low as to compare me with my sister.*

"I wouldn't have to if you did what I asked."

Just remember I came here to help you on my own accord. I didn't have to do it.

I yank at my cloak, pulling it tighter around me. "You're right. I'm sorry. But I really need you to focus right now. My friends—and also some of your dragons—need our help."

Then what are we waiting for? What's your plan?

I shake my head. As much as I appreciate Sobek's help, he's not Elan. I miss her terribly.

"I need you to talk to all of them. Maybe if the three Valkyries gather our magic and use it together, it may have enough of an effect against the giant."

Chapter Twelve

Remaining invisible, Sobek and I hover above the giant.

"What can we do, Sobek? We need to come up with a plan." I keep my voice in a whisper, hoping we're out of the giant's hearing range. Just in case, I remain alert, ready to shift if the giant searches for the origin of the talking.

I'm open to ideas. The cheek in his voice rings loud and clear, and I groan with frustration. He just doesn't know when it's inappropriate.

I clamp my teeth together to stop myself from giving a biting response. A vast void expands beneath me, giving me the feeling of floating on air as my gaze passes through Sobek's invisible form to focus on the giant. He doesn't respond in facial expression or movement, and I keep hoping we're out of his hearing range.

Tanda's red eyes remain wide with fear at being

trapped in a hand big enough to secure a dragon. Britta's jaw is set in determination, her Valkyrie training kicking in. The concentration is clear on her face as she's continually assessing the situation and possible escape options.

As my brain whirls with options, trying to develop the best plan of action, an idea rises. "Sobek. I need you to pass on the message. I need Hildr, Britta, Tanda, and Drogon to hear this as well. That way, we all know what's going on."

Okay. Here goes. Sobek clears his voice. *Um. Hi, everyone. This is Sobek.*

Tanda raises her head, her eyes searching frantically for Sobek.

Remain still, Sobek commands. *Act as though you can't hear me. Any movement you make should be slow and aimless, as though everything is as it seems.*

Both dragons, Britta, and Hildr, casually spin their heads, searching for Sobek, before refocusing on the giant.

That's better, but you won't find us. We're invisible. Kara wants me to pass on a message. We may have a chance to help Tanda and Britta escape if we all work together. Hildr and Britta, gather your magic. Let it well as large as you can. Sobek pauses, the silence piercing through the distress of having two of our own captured as we glide down to hover next to the outside of the giant's hand. *Okay. Now brace yourselves. The three Valkyries are going to shoot your magic at the giant. The magic you hold isn't enough to take down a giant of this size, so together, you're going to shoot it at the hand securing Tanda. Hildr and Britta, aim for the fingers. Tanda and Britta, get ready to flee. Let's hope this will work. On the count of three. One. Two. Three.*

All three Valkyries shoot their magic. Suddenly, the giant's hand twitches and flings open, an automatic reaction from aggravated nerves. The expected cry of pain doesn't happen. Instead, the blue giant gazes at his hand, confusion plastered on his face. Tanda scrambles to her feet, wings flapping urgently, as she pushes off and takes flight. Her unusual humped form isn't as agile as the other dragons', and she struggles more than usual with the added weight of Britta. My teeth clench, and I silently wish her luck.

The giant's reaction is slow, his massive head apparently absent of a fast-thinking brain. The puzzled gaze travels slowly over his hand, his mouth dropping open after realizing that he has released the red dragon. Slowly, his hand swings at Tanda.

"Fly left!" Britta cries.

Tanda dodges to the side, and the giant's stroke barely misses the humped dragon. Britta twists in the saddle, keeping an eye on the giant's movements.

When the giant swipes again, Britta calls, "Go right!"

My heart is beating rapidly. Tanda's rise is extremely slow, and the giant's reach barely misses her.

After searching his empty hand, the giant braces, ready to strike again. He extends his arm, raising his hand and lifting it close to where Sobek and I are hovering. Using my additional welled magic, I shoot at the back of the hand. I curse as the large amount of saved magic I release doesn't cause even a grimace on the giant's face.

The massive blue man reaches up, grasping for Tanda.

Britta screeches, "Forward!"

Tanda's wings double their pace, and she follows her rider's instruction, narrowly missing the clasp of the giant. The giant swipes his right hand, aiming for Tanda, and I clench my teeth, hoping for the best.

Britta yells, "Left!"

Tanda dodges to the left then up, and the blue fingertips narrowly miss my friends as they fly just out of reach. Drogon rises, under Hildr's instruction to greet Tanda and Britta, and I join them. Relief washes over me, and I clap, echoed by Hildr.

Dragon scales! Drogon's rough deep voice trails our clapping. *That was close.*

You don't need to tell me. Tanda's wide eyes peer below, a slight hint of triumph covering her face.

Britta gazes over Tanda's side at the large blue man, her body shaking visibly. "Let's get out of here."

Wide eyes stare up at us, and the corners of the blue mouth turn down, the sad expression on his face growing as he watches us fly higher, into the cover of the clouds. Once out of his vengeful stare, we hover, catching our breath.

Britta pulls at the bottom of her black leather top, straightening a few wrinkles, almost in a nervous gesture. "Thank you, guys. I couldn't have done it without you. Well, really, we couldn't have done it without you."

Sobek turns visible, and we hover next to them. "How did the giant catch you?" I ask.

She shrugs. "The giant appeared out of nowhere. We were searching for Naga and Eir, and before I knew it, an enormous hand clasped around Tanda from below, encasing most of us in the hold. The grasp secured me for a little while then released me slightly as he secured Tanda more. I might have been able to escape, but there was no way I was leaving Tanda alone." She rubs the red dragon under the scales in front of her saddle. "Not only do I need her, but she's also become a good friend."

Tanda's wide eyes soften, and she cranes her neck to nudge Britta's leg.

"I know what you mean." I stare down at Sobek. Many of his features are exactly the same as Elan's, except for his size and personality. Still, my heart sinks with sadness. I miss my beautiful dragon friend. Sobek's been helpful, and I know I couldn't complete this trip without him, but he's not Elan. I push the thoughts aside. My feelings toward him aren't fair. Perhaps one day, he will become a great companion for a dragon rider.

Hildr and Drogon lower to Tanda's other side, and Hildr offers a warm smile as her shaken friend's pale, freckled cheeks fill with warmth. "I'm glad we could help you. It was something the three of us had to do together. I tried throwing magic at that giant many times, and he didn't even flinch."

"Me too." I pull the cape off my head, and the cold air numbs my ears. "I stung him with magic many times, and he didn't even flinch at all. I don't think he even felt it." I scratch an arm under the golden dragon-scale sleeves. "I don't know if I should feel insulted."

Britta peers at the clouds above then circles her head, searching the area, before her eyes land on me. "Where are Eir and Naga?"

Lowering my eyes, I fiddle with the straps

attaching the saddle to Sobek. "I lost them. The giant took off so quickly that even Sobek couldn't keep up. We were doing okay until he turned a corner. By the time we got there, we couldn't find where he'd gone. The fresh snow covered his tracks. " I lift my gaze, meeting Britta's. "We have to find them. I hope the fat giant just wants to play with them and not eat them. I feel terrible that I haven't found them yet. When I heard your scream, I was in the middle of trying to find a trace of them."

"It's not your fault," Britta says. "Eir and Naga put themselves in danger."

"Yeah," Hildr grumbles. "That's Eir. Always seeing the good in people and things. Little does she think that it puts herself and others in danger. Not everything has a good heart. I love that about her, but it makes me so angry that she doesn't think otherwise."

Drogon snorts and shoots steam out of his nostrils. *Naga isn't much better.* His horned covered head turns as he lands determined brown eyes on me. *But we must find both Naga and Eir. I will miss the poor little guy. He is my little peacemaker. Always open and friendly.* He displays a long row of sharp white teeth, his draconic smile looking more threatening than friendly. *Very unlike me.*

I look from Drogon to Hildr then back to Drogon. They are well matched in personalities and trust issues, and most likely, that's why they bonded so quickly, growing mutual trust.

Breaking my thoughts, Britta says, "Let's go search for them. Perhaps if we fly at this level or just below the clouds, we might have a better chance of finding them." She pushes her long strands of hair back into place. "Now that my heart has stopped racing, I'll be able to concentrate more. I'm astounded how much my vision tunnels when my heart races."

I grin. "I think it's that way for everyone. Panic tends to make it difficult to focus." I pull my hood over my head. "I like your idea. We should leave now. They need to be found quickly in case the giant has something more sinister planned for them. There must be a reason why dragons and frost giants have been enemies for so long."

A roar reverberates up to meet us in the sky.

Chapter Thirteen

Startled, I peer over Sobek's side, checking for the disappointed giant expressing his frustration, only to find clouds below.

Sobek glances over his shoulder at me, one scaly eyebrow raised. *Jumpy much?*

Glaring at him, I'm only edged further into annoyance as he reciprocates with a playful gleam dancing in his golden-brown eyes. I stick my tongue out and tighten my cloak around my waist, straightening it to cover every inch of the saddle and my legs.

While still visible, I address the others. "Sobek and I will turn invisible and drop below the clouds to get our bearings. Wait here out of the giant's sight. We'll be back in a minute."

Sobek raises both his wings and drops beneath me as he phases into invisibility. My stomach lurches to my throat, and my heart thumps against my rib cage as I'm again flooded with the sensation of falling to my death. The wind pushes up, blowing my hood from my head. My teeth chatter from the cold and the adrenaline as I clamp one hand around the reins and grasp for the hood with the other. When we break through the cloud cover, Sobek extends his wings, and we jerk to a halt, my stomach slamming back into my abdomen.

"Thanks for the warning," I mutter to Sobek.

I can see the edges of his toothy grin from my saddle. My nerves calm after a couple of deep breaths, allowing me to get my bearings and establish the giant's location. Within a few minutes, I spot the cluster of mountains surrounding a plain in the distance. The snow had made it difficult to see where we had been before.

Pulling on the reins, I spin Sobek in that direction. "Is that the mountain cluster we were at?"

It certainly is. I'd recognize that anywhere. It's a strange formation for mountains to be that close and circling a plain. Without instruction, he ascends to meet the others. The rise is much smoother than the descent, and as we near the group, Sobek's visible golden form appears beneath me.

Indicating the direction of the mountain cluster hidden below the clouds, I say, "We're sure the giant took Eir and Naga that way. I think we should stay above the clouds for a little way. The thin giant that held Tanda and Britta remains not far from here."

Sobek leads the way over the mountains. I shiver and pull my cloak tighter around me, pulling the hood to cover my ears. Every time I use this cloak, I'm thankful I made it, especially in climates like this. I feel for Hildr and Britta, wearing only their fighting leathers. After flying for a while, Sobek gradually drops through the clouds, allowing the others to follow.

A bird's-eye view of Jotunheim spreads below us, and Sobek spreads his wings, gliding just below the clouds. I scan the area, searching for any giants or signs of our friends. The giant we left behind is too far to spot, and I see no sign of other giants in the area. The two dragons with Hildr and Britta follow. Silence encompasses us, everyone deep in thought while scanning for any danger or our peaceful friends.

The golden dragon slows his pace, allowing the others to catch up, and they spread out slightly, widening the search. The icy land's blueness makes it harder to spot the threat of blue giants and a similar-colored dragon.

Glancing over my shoulder, I notice the others have fallen behind. I call over my shoulder, pointing down at the familiar plain stretching before us. "This is where we lost them. The giant headed off into this plain. By the time we reached it, he had disappeared. I'm assuming he went down one of the gaps between the mountains." I pull on Sobek's reins to slow him, and the other dragons labor to catch up. "We searched down every single gap between the mountains, but we didn't see any sign of the giant or evidence of where he had traveled."

Drogon reaches Sobek's side first. "We should spread out around the circle, concentrating on individual sections, and see if we can spot anything farther out," Hildr suggests as Britta and Tanda join us.

We part ways, and I travel straight across the plain to the far side of the mountains, while Hildr and Drogon part to the left and Tanda and Britta search the right. The terrain in front of us remains void of evidence that any giant, dragon, or Valkyrie has passed through.

"Sobek, can you contact the other dragons to see if they've had any luck?"

Only a moment later, Sobek responds, *No. They haven't seen anything, either, the riders or their dragons.* He veers slightly to one side, and we search the mountains below.

Dragon communication is such a useful thing, I muse, wishing communication with the other Valkyries was that easy. "Can you call Naga and see if he can hear you? If he's close, maybe he will be able to direct us to their location."

Sobek groans. *Why didn't we think of this before? It would have saved so much time.*

"Dragon speech isn't my first language. It doesn't come naturally to me to expect others to hear me over a mile away," I say mockingly. "More likely, why didn't you think of it?"

It's not exactly my first language, either.

I frown, but before I can ask his meaning, my thoughts are interrupted by his call dragging my attention back to the task on hand.

Naga? Sobek's voice echoes in my head.

I wait patiently, hoping for an answer.

Naga? Can you hear me, Naga?

The silence eats at my nerves as we fly farther, searching.

As minutes pass and more distance is devoured underneath us, Sobek keeps calling out, *Naga? Can you hear me?*

Tanda and Drogon join in the calls, their voices sounding in my head, the distance making them fainter than Sobek's. With each dragon calling for Naga, I hope one of them will be close enough for Naga to hear us.

The combined effort is invigorating, and I long to

join in and call out for Naga and Eir, but I resist the urge. My efforts would be fruitless, compared to the dragons'. My voice would be lost in the icy breeze, which cuts through every gap in my cape. At least the dragons have voices that can't be affected by outside elements, although they are possibly dimmed by the thickness of the rocks. I kick myself at the thought. Mountains are filled with rocks and caves. Even the dragons' voices were probably dimmed.

"Sobek, can you fly lower and circle each mountain in the area while calling out to Naga? If we spot any caves, you might need to descend and call through the entrance."

But Naga should be able to hear me from here. Sobek sounds confused.

"Yes, Naga should be able to hear you, but the rocks and the mountains would be dense and harder for your voice to break through even though it is done telepathically." I'm puzzled that this didn't occur to Sobek, but I push the thought away when I observe the actions of the other two dragons. They aren't lowering and calling into every cave either. "Isn't that right?"

Even though Sobek is flying, his shoulders slump forward slightly. *Yes, it is right. It makes sense now.* He descends and flies closer to the mountains, his voice projecting every time we see a gap or cave. His calls for Naga grow more agitated every minute that passes without progress. *Naga? Naga, where are you?*

We pass another mountain.

Naga. Naga, can you hear me? Sobek flaps his large golden-membraned wings, aiming for the next mountain and calls again.

A small voice echoes back in my head. *Yes. Yes, Naga can hear you.* The sound is music to my ears—so soft and frail yet still sweet.

Sobek's wings halt, almost reversing, before he circles to the previous mountain and calls again, *Naga? Where are you, Naga?*

Naga... Naga don't know. His broken English sounds slightly louder. *The giant took us somewhere. Naga couldn't see. Big hands were wrapped around Naga, blocking Naga's eyes by his massive fingers.* A soft grunt of frustration sounds through the telepathy. *I shall ask Eir.* We were left in silence for a few moments until Naga came back. *Eir doesn't know either. She says we have been brought to some mountain. She doesn't know which one. They all looked the same, and we passed so many, and the giant covered the distance quickly.*

The vulnerability in Naga's small voice pulls at my heartstrings as Sobek flies around the mountain, looking for an opening big enough for a frost giant. Abruptly he halts outside a deep tunnel into the closest mountain. It's quite large, probably big enough for a giant to travel through.

Sobek turns invisible, and we land in front of the entrance, his talons soft against the stone. We peer deep into the tunnel, shocked by the depth at which the hole sinks into the mountain and disappears into the earth below.

"I don't like this, Sobek. There could be anything down there. It's a big enough tunnel for any frost giant come through. I don't know how we didn't see it before." I shift nervously in the saddle. "I think we should let the others know where we are first before we go down. We might need backup."

Suddenly, we push off into the sky. The golden scales appear underneath me, and Sobek raises his head before projecting his voice. *Are you guys ever going to catch up? You need to come this way. You will find us at the end of the plain, off to the right. We've followed Naga's voice, and hopefully, we've tracked it to the right place.*

No need to be rude about it. We're on our way, Drogon grumbles, his voice sounding closer.

We need you to come help out, in case we're ambushed. I thought you guys would have been here already. Surely, you would have heard me talking to Naga. Sobek's sarcasm surprises me. *Where's the red dragon?*

I'm with Drogon, Tanda says, also sounding annoyed. *We'll be there in a few minutes.*

Peering over my shoulder, I spot both Drogon and Tanda heading in our direction. Without waiting, the golden dragon sinks and lands at the tunnel entrance, followed moments later by the other dragons.

About time you guys got here.

"Sobek!" I scold. "That's rude. We could hardly hear Naga. How do you expect them to hear him?"

Glowering, Drogon lands with Hildr frowning on his back. His restraint is admirable as he ignores Sobek's comment and lifts his nose, sucking in a large breath, his nostrils constricting from the pressure. *I can small Naga. He is down this hole.*

"Great!" I say sarcastically as Tanda lands next to Drogon.

"Just what we need. Another enclosed area that's possibly a trap." Britta sighs.

Mounted, we slowly descend the tunnel, the dragons laboring to keep their footsteps silent.

Chapter Fourteen

Darkness encases us as we progress down into the tunnel, setting my nerves on edge. My eyes take a long time to adjust, and I'm thankful the dragons have better night vision.

"Where is Eir with her light-making abilities when you need her?" I murmur quietly to my friends, hoping my voice won't be heard any farther past their ears.

"What do you mean?" Hildr's whisper is barely audible.

My brows push together in a frown. I'm surprised Hildr doesn't know this. I've hardly seen Eir, compared to Hildr and Britta. "Eir has mastered how to hold light in her palm. It came in handy when we were looking for Loki."

"She's full of surprises, isn't she?" Hildr turns to Britta. "Did you know that?"

"No. But I did know she was working on magic that was more peaceful than what we would use."

Hildr huffs. "How do you know more about her than I do?"

Britta shakes her head. "I wouldn't say I know more about her. But I probably listen to her peaceful ways more than you."

"What do you mean?" Offense laces Hildr's voice. "I like Eir. I listen to her all the time."

"But you tune out when she talks about peaceful things." Britta chuckles softly. "You're too busy wanting to fight everything, always grabbing for your sword hilt."

I chuckle with Britta, knowing it to be the truth. "Clearly, you guys have been busy while I've been under Thor's guidance."

"Yeah, busy fighting." Britta glares at Hildr, the look only barely captured in the light fading from the entrance.

Hildr spreads her arms. "We don't fight much."

"What are you talking about?" Britta's eyebrows rise in surprise, along with her volume. "Eir doesn't. But we fight all the time. You just don't see it as fighting because it's not the way you prefer… with a sword or sparring."

"Shhh!" I try to quiet them, the request falling on deaf ears.

"I don't like to fight all the time." Hildr plants her fists on her hips and faces me. "Do I, Kara?"

I pull at the leather around my neck. "Well, I haven't hung around with you lately. But you do like a good confrontation, whether it be in battle or with words." I try to keep my voice a whisper.

"Fine!" Hildr huffs. "Take Britta's side." The leather of her uniform squeaks as she folds her arms, the motion barely visible from the almost extinguished light.

"You're biting well today, Hildr." Amusement sparkles in Britta's voice. "A little bit more argumentative than usual."

A large grumble sounds from down the tunnel, breaking up our conversation. The only sound remaining is the soft patter of the dragons' paws gently stepping on the stone as they progress through the tunnel. I feel the pressure of Sobek's wings tucking closer to his body, and I try to move with the sway of his movements to eliminate the squeaking of my leather uniform and saddle.

The noise from below sounds again, and with it, I imagine the giant scattering boulders and clashing them into each other—my nerves fire, stretching them to their limit.

The soft noise coming from our group still feels too loud. I wouldn't be surprised if the sound escalates as it travels farther down the tunnel. Straining my eyes, I try to see more in front of us, only to be disappointed. With my sight failing to pick up anything, I'm left feeling glad that the dragons can see in the dark.

After several more steps, the dragons round a corner, and a dull light glows in the distance. Eventually, my vision improves, revealing the three dragons' outlines and eventually Hildr's and Britta's faces. Sobek disappears from my sight, and I set to work making sure my dragon-scale cloak completely covers the saddle and me. Peering out from under the hood, I catch sight of Hildr. Her jaw clenches, and the muscles along her neck and jawline ripple with force. She looks as though she is steeling her emotions. On the other side, Britta seems slightly more relaxed.

Sobek's voice projects through my head. *Naga?* After a short pause, he tries again. *Naga, are you in this cave?*

A little squeal sounds in my head. *Yes. Naga and Eir is here in this cave. We are here with the giant. Naga started a fire for him. The giant asked Naga to.*

A combined sigh of relief escapes my friends. Naga would have sounded more panicked if things weren't right. I smile. Naga's language skills have improved significantly over the last couple of years, but he still refers to himself in the third person. Suddenly, a chill runs down my spine. Although Naga sounded positive, a deep fear fills me as I think of the fire Naga happily started for the giant. Maybe it was intended to cook them later.

My thoughts are interrupted by Naga's voice. *The giant's happy for the fire Naga made. He can warm his hands.*

A curse escapes Britta's lips, and I study her pale face as we continue forward as slowly and as silently as possible. I can't help wondering if Britta's thoughts match my own.

Loud banging from the end of the tunnel interrupts my thoughts, and I stiffen as a soft, panicked voice that sounds awfully like Eir's cries, "What are you doing?"

Absent an answer, more loud bangs follow, like large logs of wood being thrown on the fire.

The giant's voice booms. "I'm stacking up the fire. It must be strong and burning. It's the only way I can cook my dinner."

The tunnel fills with more sounds of logs thrown on the fire.

"And what are you going to cook?" Eir's voice remains tense, almost at a level of panic.

I nudge Sobek to move faster. Knots twist in my stomach as I wait for the giant's answer.

When it doesn't come, Eir continues, "I don't see anything in here to cook."

A deep belly chuckle lined with an evil tone reverberates down the tunnel, and my cheeks turn clammy.

"Why, after I finish playing with you, I will eat you. You can go first because you will cook quicker and stop me from being so hungry. But I will enjoy the dragon better. He will fill my tummy much more. You're too bony, and your body doesn't hold much meat. I have a big belly to fill."

The following cackle doesn't ease my nerves. My fear has come true.

Did you hear that, Sobek? Naga's voice, soft and scared, fills my head.

We all heard that, Drogon answers before Sobek can. *We are coming. Don't worry. We'll be there soon.*

Please do. Eir looks very scared, just like Naga feels, and Naga can't stop him. He's big. You need to be here now. His fire is burning bright. Oh, what has Naga done?

A rumble sounds down the tunnel, like rocks scattering.

An internal squeak sounds from Naga. *He's getting up. He's walking toward Eir.*

A tremendous growl reaches us from deep in the tunnel, the strange, menacing sound of a ferocious dragon, but the only dragon that we know of in the tunnel is Naga, who doesn't usually sound like that.

Naga will not let you have Eir. Naga's voice sounds oddly aggressive, a deep, low growl. It's extremely out of character, but the peaceful dragon has no other choice.

Drogon throws his large spiky head forward, expelling a loud roar that echoes down the tunnel. I shoot an impressed look toward him, but it's missed entirely because all I spot is his behind as he charges forward. He seems to have taken charge of the dragons since Elan isn't here. Usually, this would be a task undertaken by another emperor dragon—not a role Sobek has seemed keen to uphold even though he's directly related to Elan and Eingana, leader of the dragons. Before I know it, Tanda sprints after Drogon with Britta egging her on.

Frustrated by Sobek's lack of response after a few seconds, I kick his sides then jolt magic under his scales, enough to get the message through. "What are you doing, Sobek? Go! We have to help."

Without another word, Sobek breaks into a run, following the other dragons' lead.

Chapter Fifteen

Tanda struggles to keep up with Drogon. The brown dragon's talons scrape over the rocks as he charges straight toward the light at the end. All attempts to sneak up are tossed away in seconds. The giant will be fully aware that we're coming now.

The light from the fire frames Drogon's intimidating horned head as he springs to ram it straight at the enormous giant. Hildr screams her Valkyrie cry. The high-pitched sound is disturbing as it echoes down the tunnel. The noise intensifies as Britta joins Hildr, holding her sword in one hand and the saddle straps in the other. The longest of Drogon's horns barely pierces the giant's abdomen before the giant swings a fist in an undercut at him. Hildr sees it coming and pulls on his straps, yanking his head back, dragging the horn across the giant's tunic and leaving a long tear. Blood seeps through the damage, and the giant cries out in pain and frustration, his fist narrowly missing the brown dragon. Britta circles the giant on Tanda and jabs her sword into the giant's butt cheek. The massive hips jerk forward as he cries out in disapproval.

Sobek and I follow the others into the cave, our pace slower as we use the guise of invisibility to assess the situation. Naga and Eir remain at the back of the cave, their mouths wide as they observe the commotion. Using Hildr and Britta's distraction, we veer to the right and use the fire's light to observe the giant's captives, checking them for any injuries. My heart soars as they seem unscathed, and my attention quickly turns to the attack on the giant.

Sobek charges to the fire and leans over it. I'm puzzled at his sudden interest until I hear a sucking sound and see the red-and-orange flames dwindle away. The embers sputter for a brief second before recouping, but not before Sobek shifts underneath me and we rise from the ground. The movement feels as though he's stretching his neck up. Flames shoot from the spot I imagine his mouth is, straight at the frost giant's face. The giant recoils from the fire, ducking and releasing a cry of shock as the plume shoots overhead from an invisible source. The giant's shrieks echo down the tunnel, twisting knots in my stomach. Even though the giant wants to hurt my friends, I hate the thought of inflicting pain.

Sobek's body lowers underneath me and trudges to the fire. Once again, the flames flicker as an enormous amount of the bonfire disappears with a sucking sound. This time, after a pause, a strange vibration runs down his neck then recoils. His head jerks forward, and he regurgitates embers at the giant's hands then feet. This fire seems thicker and more than what usually comes out of Elan. It has more volume, and the stream appears longer—perhaps it's a combination of dragon flame and the fire from the bonfire.

Drogon springs off the ground, and Hildr screeches a Valkyrie cry accentuated by the enclosed walls of the cave as she clings to the reins with one hand and her sword in the other. The brown dragon flaps his wings, rising then spinning to pummel his spiky tail into the blue giant's face. I cringe as the spikes pierce into the blue cheek. Drogon recoils, and Hildr bends to the side, slicing the other blue cheek with her sword.

The giant sweeps his hands, trying to avoid the long mace-like tail, only to be distracted by the cut from Hildr's sword. The brown dragon's tail careens straight into the large eye, embedding deep into the socket. My stomach convulses, its contents rising in protest over what the three dragons are doing to the giant. His screeches overpower the high-pitched

Valkyrie cries. A huge blue hand covers the injured eye when the spiky tail is removed. Tanda lines up to join Drogon as Hildr and Britta set to work, shooting magic in unison at the giant's hands and eyes, changing targets when they think of another weak spot.

The giant shrieks, falling against the wall before hoisting himself off the hard surface, arms flailing and feet stomping, narrowly missing the fire as he scrambles down the tunnel. Cries echo as he stumbles and trips over large boulders that block his way, the hand not covering the injured eye fumbling along the walls as he tries to get out of the cave.

Drogon braces himself on all fours and roars after the giant.

The giant's cry answers as his voice echoes behind him as he continues to bungle his way to the entrance. "I don't like dragons anymore. They're not cute. They aren't fun to play with. Stop it, dragons! You're hurting me."

Sobek's invisible form bounces to face the fire, and I gasp as the flames halve then splutter and cough in protest.

The sickness in my stomach churns. "Stop it, Sobek. Surely, that's enough. The giant is running away, screaming. We have defended Eir and Naga. We don't need to attack him again."

But his noise may alert other giants. You must stop him, Sobek says.

Sobek is right. I know he is. I swallow, pushing the contents of my stomach back down and straighten my shoulders. I'm a Valkyrie. I need to toughen up. A lack of battles has softened me. We're fighting for our lives and the lives of our friends. This mission can't fail, or lives on Asgard will also be in danger. "All right! Let's make sure that doesn't happen."

As Sobek sucks in more flames, Eir's face falls in horror. Her hand reaches for his invisible form, and she screeches, "No! Stop! You don't need to go any farther. We're safe." She runs to the tunnel, holding her arms out wide, attempting to stop any more attacks on the giant.

Slowly, Tanda approaches and stands over the top of the peaceful Valkyrie. The dragon's glowing red eyes gleam down at Eir, and her voice, cold and laced with disapproval, travels through our heads. *The giants must be punished for what they did to us. A giant was going to kill Britta and me as well. You should be stronger. You're a Valkyrie.* The red dragon puffs out a mixture of smoke and steam all over Eir. She flicks her long red tail, sending the white tuft of fur on the end flinging around the room. The brilliant red wings spread wide as though she's contemplating taking off after the giant even against Eir's disapproval. Suddenly, a brown streak flies past the red dragon, gliding down the tunnel, releasing a roar of warning toward the fleeing giant. The spiky brown dragon seems unstoppable with his war-hungry Valkyrie on his back, sword drawn.

No. Drogon, no. A sweet, innocent voice fills our heads as we watch Drogon disappear. *Stop doing this. This is not nice. You make Naga sad.*

I search the cave until my eyes land on Naga. His big blue eyes are drooping with sadness, and my heart wants to break.

Sobek's feet grind to a halt, and a thump sounds down the tunnel, followed by the clacking of rocks.

Drogon appears on the other side of Eir, a strange mixture of emotions running over his scaly face. *Sorry, Naga. I was caught up in rage. That giant threatened to eat my friends.*

Eir lowers her arms, and Tanda joins Drogon.

Sobek appears underneath me and pauses before passing the peaceful Valkyrie and gazing over his shoulder. *Come, Naga. Let us leave.*

Naga's little round face nods once, and Eir climbs onto his back. Contemplation covers their faces as they follow us in silence.

Tanda circles around Sobek and approaches Naga, nudging Eir then Naga with her head as she walks along beside them. *I'm sorry.* She focuses on Eir. *Fear for myself and for my friends took over. We're all sorry. We were frightened for you both, and we wanted to make sure this giant left. Perhaps after the scare we gave him, he will tell the other giants to leave us alone.*

Naga cranes his neck to gaze up into Tanda's fiery red eyes. *Naga was scared—this is true. And Eir was too. But we live in peace. There is no reason to act like you did.*

Drogon snorts. *But the giant was going to eat you.*

Naga's eyes widen with fear. *Yes. The giant did try to eat Eir and Naga. We are grateful that you saved us.* Naga bows his head in a display of respect to their rescuers. *He is gone now, and we are safe. Let's leave him alone. He is already hurt, and this makes Naga and Eir sad.*

I gaze at the blue dragon and his rider. Both want peace and honor among dragons and Valkyries alike. Their love for other creatures is bountiful. We could all learn from them. Even after their life was threatened, they still want to uphold peace and the hope that good exists in other beings.

"Oh, Vanir!" Hildr's voice echoes down the tunnel.

I spin to see what's wrong. The entrance of the tunnel frames Drogon and Hildr with a background of nothing but darkness.

"How did it become night so quickly?" Hildr throws her arms out at the sides, disappointment

117

covering her face. "I swear it was daylight less than half an hour ago, without a hint of nighttime coming."

Sobek joins them at the entrance, his nostrils working overtime, trying to pick up scents and assessing the land before us. Hovering slightly over the horizon, the moon shines dully, the light just touching the land's surface.

The little blue dragon stops next to Sobek, and his big blue eyes appear larger in the faint light as he gazes at me then at the golden dragon. *What are we going to do?*

Chapter Sixteen

B ritta groans. "Great! We're stuck in Jotunheim at night with hardly any moonlight. It's impossible to see."

Tanda surveys the horizon from behind my shoulder. "So what's the plan?" Hot breath covers my head and neck, a welcome warmth to my body, which is riddled to the bone with cold despite having donned my dragon-scale cloak.

I observe the countryside, taking in the extent of darkness, pondering what to do next. "I wasn't expecting darkness to settle so quickly. I didn't realize we had taken so long to find Eir and Naga after rescuing you and Britta. I was so preoccupied with finding them that I lost track of time."

Eir gasps. "Wait. You had to rescue Tanda and Britta too?"

I nod then realize she probably can't see me. "Yes. That's another reason why Tanda was so upset, but that's a story for a different time." I rub my upper arm, missing the warmth of Tanda's breath. "It's too dark for the Valkyries to see. Either we rely on the dragons to lead the way, or we rest here and hope the frost giant doesn't return."

Drogon snorts. *Oh, the frost giant won't be returning. I'm pretty sure I sent a clear message.*

"I'm pretty exhausted." Eir yawns audibly. "That took a fair bit out of me."

"I think it took a fair bit out of all of us," Britta agrees.

The decision weighing heavy on me, I roll my shoulders then my neck, attempting to ease the tension and clear my mind. "We need to leave Jotunheim as soon as possible." I gaze down the tunnel, remembering the warmth of the fire in the distance and the cave's shelter from this harsh land. A chilly breeze catches me from outside, and I return my gaze to the darkness covering the frosty land. "But I don't like the looks of it out there. Unless the dragons can read a map, maybe we should stay here for a bit and wait for the moon to rise enough to shine some light over the land."

Nope. I definitely can't read a map, Drogon answers.

"Then we need to wait for more light so I can read the map. If I don't follow Thor's directions, we'll probably get lost, and it's going to take us longer to find Angrboda."

Sobek drops to his haunches, and I climb off his saddle, the clomp of my boots echoing down the tunnel. Another gust blows from the land, and I shiver, tugging the edges of my cloak closer together. "Let's move deeper for a while and have something to eat." The cold breeze encases my hands as I reach for the saddlebag and carry it to the middle of the tunnel. "Here should be far enough inside the cave to give us some shelter from the wind yet also allow the dragons to keep an eye on the entrance for any giants."

Unpacking the supplies, I hand each Valkyrie some food then sit on the hard stone floor, resting my back against Sobek's warm body. "I think it's best for us to rest for a while in the cave." I take a bite of the dried meat, the shock of its saltiness causing my tongue to recoil until the taste spreads through my mouth. "You three and your dragons can rest around the fire."

Hildr starts to protest, and I cut her off.

"It's no use all of us being tired. I'm sure Eir and Naga could use some rest, as well as Britta and Tanda. You and Drogon can be the last line of defense if anything gets past Sobek and me."

Sobek snorts out steam. *What about my rest?*

"Are you for real?" I ask.

I'm tired too. Hot, smoky breath washes over me as I imagine him yawning.

"Then you can sleep near me at the entrance of the tunnel with half an eye open. That should be enough for a dragon to regain their strength. I need you close in case I need backup." I prop myself up to stand and feel for the cool firm roundness of apples in my pack. Then I fumble around the circle in the darkness to hand one to every Valkyrie. "These are fresh from Midgard this morning—courtesy of Thor." I then hand out chunks of bread from the palace kitchens.

"It must be nice to be able to eat from Thor's supplies," Britta says, followed by a loud crunch into an apple.

My thumb strokes the firm skin of the apple in my hand, my mouth watering in anticipation. "I must admit it's nice having my meals cooked for me by the palace cooks. This is a perk, but you guys keep it real for me. After all, I still live with you in our humble accommodations."

"Aw! I pity you," Britta chimes in.

A small ball of flame races in midair down the tunnel from the cave. When I brace myself to move away from the attacking light, it suddenly halts and slowly moves to hover over the middle of Eir's upraised palm.

I watch her fondle the flame, mesmerized how she appears to be caressing it like a favorite pet. Eventually, I blink, bringing my attention back to the conversation. "Well, it's going to be worse if I don't fix this mess with Loki. I might have all my privileges cut off. Then I'll be eating back with you as well. I may even have to cook for myself."

Sobek scoffs, his lips blowing an unintentional raspberry.

"Hey!" I say with feigned hurt. "That doesn't seem nice. What's your problem?"

Eir giggles. "And we all know how bad your cooking is." Her eyes gleam with mischief in the light of the flame.

I glare at her, adding as much malice as I can, only to be rewarded by her chuckle growing louder, joined by Hildr and Britta.

"It's funny because it's true." Hildr holds her stomach.

"Your cooking isn't much better," I retort.

Hildr waves a hand at me dismissively. "Do you think I care?" She wipes the edges of her eyes. "The specialty that I focus on is not cooking—it's fighting. You should know that by now."

"Yeah. Thank goodness we have Eir to cook." Britta puffs, regaining some air.

A loud clatter of rocks reverberates down the

tunnel, and we fall into silence. With wide eyes, we look at one another. The ground vibrates slightly as the sound of giant footsteps comes from outside. I reprimand myself as we wait in anticipation, knowing we were too noisy.

Several more footsteps echo down the tunnel until they slowly fade away.

"We have to keep it down," I whisper. "We let our caution slip and made too much noise. I think it's time to break up. You lot go down into the cave like we discussed and get some rest. Sobek and I will head to the entrance. At least if you talk down there, it won't be so loud. But try to get some rest. I'll keep an eye out here and let you know when we have enough light to read the map and see the land."

Quietly, the Valkyries pack up, and we part ways, the dragons following like personal bodyguards, the sway of their hips outlined by the dull light in Eir's hand.

"Come, Sobek," I whisper before creeping quietly to the tunnel entrance. I pull my hood over my head and tighten the cloak around my body, securing it to stop the chilly breeze from seeping through my clothes. I park myself on the cold, hard stone ground on one side of the entrance with my back against the rock, watching the darkness and waiting for any sounds.

The cloak keeps out most of the cold breeze and traps enough warmth that I'm not disappointed when Sobek sits on the other side of the tunnel. The whites of his golden-brown eyes barely shine under the dull moonlight as his eyes search the surrounding area.

Sinking my teeth into the juicy apple as slowly and quietly as I can, I tear away a mouthful. At the crispy sound, I cringe, hoping the noise doesn't carry too far. I keep my eyes and ears peeled for any attraction to the noise.

By the time I've finished eating, a small rumble comes from the other side of the entrance. Quietly, I approach Sobek to find his eyes closed and his head resting on his extended front talons. When I brush my hand over his nostrils, he works his mouth then stretches, extending his legs farther and tucking his tail around his body. He seems to be in a deep sleep. The speed of his slumber surprises me, yet I leave him to rest. The day has been long for all of us.

Circling back, I slump against the cold stone wall and let my knees crumple beneath me. The sleeping golden dragon's scales glimmer dully in the faint moonlight. The sight sparkles in my peripheral vision as I keep watch. His steady breaths slow to a monotone beat, dragging out and setting off a slight rumble deep in his throat with the sound of intense sleep.

Leaning back against the cold stones, I adjust my cloak, making sure every gap is covered. The leather-lined golden-scale cloak traps the warmth I need, making me grateful for the time I spent making it. My boots stick out the bottom, and a chill travels up my legs. I hug my knees to my chest, covering them with the cloak. Warm, I stare out into the darkness, and time seems to stand still. The moon's ascent is slow. What little it illuminates catches my attention until I know no threats are out there. As hardly anything moves and nothing needs my attention, the boredom causes my alertness to fade and my eyelids to grow heavy, weighing down my eyes until they shut.

My body convulses, and I start, realizing that my head fell to the side with a jerk that woke me up. I fling my eyes wide and stand, stretching my body, then pace the entrance. Angry with myself for falling asleep, I push the hood of my cloak back, allowing the cold air to flood my face, waking my senses. I'm supposed to be guarding everyone, not sleeping on the job.

A noise sounds around the right corner of the entrance, and I halt in the middle of the cave. I attempt to peer around the corner while trying to stay hidden, twisting my body into an awkward angle, but I can't spot anything amiss. Not wanting to face whatever it is alone, I search for the sleeping Sobek, only to find the spot empty. My heart stops beating. Thoughts of him being nabbed by a giant run through my head, which would all be my fault because I fell asleep, leaving the place unguarded. Elan would be so disappointed in me. I rub my temples, attempting to drum up reason. Keeping my steps silent and trying not to alert whatever was around the side of the tunnel, I approach the place I last saw the dragon. Perhaps he turned invisible for added protection because he was worried his golden scales were glimmering too brightly in the moonlight. With my arms out, I search for an invisible sleeping dragon. Maybe I'll wake him up by falling over him. The thought sparks a slight amusement and lack of empathy. I shrug. It's time he woke up.

Sweeping my feet forward, I take cautious steps, determined not to fall flat on my face into a scaled dragon side or the hard stones. I continue until I reach the far side of the entrance and my hands land on the cold stone wall, unobstructed. A deep chill sets into my bones. Sobek's gone.

Chapter Seventeen

"Sobek!" My voice is a hoarse whisper. "Sobek. Are you around?"

Pausing to concentrate, I hope for some dreaming noises or a dragon voice in my head, confirming he is nearby in his invisible form. Remaining alert, I peel my eyes, hoping for a golden dragon to suddenly appear in front of me. No matter how hard I try, I can't think of why he would leave, but then again, I don't know him that well. I thought I had only dozed off for a couple of minutes. Now that I can't find Sobek, I'm not so sure.

Quickly, I pad through the tunnel, softly calling Sobek's name, hoping it's quiet enough to not echo out of the tunnel and into the lands of Jotunheim. The large tunnel is eerie in a different way from the one that leads to Gilroma's cave, and the hairs on the back of my neck stand on end as I pass through the darkness. I reach the cave at the end. All the other dragons and Valkyries are resting peacefully against their partners, their bodies relaxed in a deep sleep. I see no sign of the golden dragon anywhere.

Quickly, I race back to the entrance of the cave. The last thing I need is for something to sneak into the cave without me knowing. My trek lacks a golden dragon, and I call again, "Sobek!"

Only the whistling winds outside the cave answer me.

"Sobek, where are you?"

Lacking a response, I step outside the cave, and my nose instantly freezes in the icy breeze. Despite the wind, I leave the hood slightly back, making sure it doesn't block any part of my vision. Tugging at the ends of the sleeves, I bury my hands within its protection. Moving away from the shelter of the tunnel, I land in the light of the moon, and my heart sinks. The dragon scales covering my cloak are glowing in the moonlight, basically calling out to any giant to come and find me. With sincere regret, I untie the belt and shrug it off, folding it and tucking it in the bag that held the food. My body aches, screaming for the cloak's comfort and protection from these cold winds, but I press forward, trying to ignore that.

Hunching over and rubbing my forearms, I scan the sky for a golden dragon. No shadows pass above, and no golden scales glimmer in the moonlight. My search continues on the ground as I survey every spot of the land more visible in the stronger moon-light. We probably should be continuing our journey, but we can't go without Sobek. Elan wouldn't forgive me if I left him here even if he left without me knowing.

I'm conscious that I am still the guardian of my friends, and keeping an eye on the tunnel proves challenging while I'm searching for a rogue dragon. I pass the edge of a mountain, and something golden catches my eye. The breeze stills for a moment, and I hear chuckling. I frown. That's not the sound I was expecting in the middle of the night, and the noise doesn't sound like a frost giant. The gold glimmers.

"Sobek?"

The dragon twists to look at me, the scales on his face twisted in an expression of curiosity followed by amusement. Over his shoulder, something red catches my eye, and I frown as my eyes connect with the beady eyes of a squirrel, glaring down at me over his pointy nose.

"Ratatoskr?" I ask. "What are you doing here?"

The squirrel's body shakes as he climbs off the icy mountainside and onto Sobek's shoulder and tucks his little feet under one of Sobek's scales and against the soft skin underneath.

"Oh, Sobek. You're so warm." The squirrel's high-pitched nasal voice sounds strange in the silence. "I can finally feel my toes."

"Ratatoskr. What are you doing here?" I ask again.

"Oh, Kara. I didn't see you there," the squirrel lies, making me clench my jaw. "Sobek and I are having a little chat."

I eye them both suspiciously and cross my arms. "Sobek is supposed to be guarding the cave to help protect my friends and me. Why are you out here, Sobek?" I raise an eyebrow.

Ratatoskr runs along Sobek's back and whispers something into the dragon's ear. Sobek snorts with laughter, and the squirrel returns to his original spot on the dragon's shoulder. I glower, only to be met by Sobek's mischievous grin, which irks me. I shove the annoyance aside. Clearly, I need some sleep. I'm getting agitated over stupid things.

I heard a little noise, and I went out to investigate. Imagine my surprise when I spotted Ratatoskr freezing his little tail off, here in Jotunheim. I've only been here for a moment.

"But I've been looking for you for the last ten minutes, at least." I spread my arms in frustration.

It took me a moment to find Ratatoskr, Sobek retorts cheekily.

Pulling my eyes away from Sobek, I observe the squirrel with a glare. "And why are you here, Ratatoskr? You still haven't answered me."

The red fur ball moves to the top of Sobek's head and leans against a horn, tucking his feet back into the dragon's scales, then plants a hand on his hip. "Actually, I was looking for you."

Sobek attempts to gaze up at Ratatoskr, confusion and amusement written on his face.

The squirrel continues, "I have a message for you from Loki."

"Oh." Bewilderment flushes through me as my gaze scans Sobek then Ratatoskr, thinking they look way too chummy to be looking for me.

"Yeah. I have a message for you from Loki," he says again, nodding as though satisfied with his answer.

I think I catch amusement on Sobek's face, but his expression changes before I can read it.

"Yeah," the squirrel repeats as though trying to convince me. "That's right." He crosses his arms over his chest.

I scratch the back of my head. "Have you found Loki?"

"Of course. I wouldn't just be making up his

message." The squirrel manages to look offended. "It wouldn't be worth my while."

Shrugging, I wait for the message to be delivered, bracing myself for an insult. "Well, don't just stand there. Tell me."

"Yeah. All right. Here goes. Loki says that if you really wanted to find him, you already would have."

Gasping, I spread my arms out to the sides in frustration. "How am I supposed to find him? He disappeared, running away when he was in my care, leaving me to take the blame for his actions. Having success in locating him is like finding a needle in a haystack. He can turn into any form he likes. I can't believe he said that!" I throw my head back in frustration. "You give him a little, and he takes a mile," I rant, unable to help myself.

Ratatoskr raises a furry eyebrow. "Well, he says that he's been in your face the whole time. You could have found him, but you're too complacent. He said that the number of opportunities he's given you is ridiculous, and he's starting to wonder if there's anything in your brain." The squirrel passes on the message with such conviction that it's insulting.

"Ergh! I'm not stupid. Loki hasn't been near me. If he has, the shape he took on would have made it impossible to tell it was him." I flail my arms. "He could have been in any form."

The smirks grow on the squirrel's and Sobek's faces.

"You hear that, Sobek? She says he could have been in any form."

They both chuckle, Sobek's belly jiggling with laughter.

Crossing my arms over my chest, I lean on one leg. "I'm glad you two find it funny. You're no better than me, Sobek." I return my glare to the squirrel. "At least we're here to seek Loki's mistress and the mother of his monstrous children. We've come across nothing but trouble on this trip. It is Loki's fault that we're here, trying to see if anyone can control his wayward offspring. They want to attack Asgard because they're angry at all of us for locking Loki up." As Sobek continues to laugh, I glare and throw in an insult. "If Sobek was as good as his sister, we could have returned home by now."

Ratatoskr elbows Sobek's head. "You see, Sobek? These are the sort of messages I like to carry. The reactions are priceless! Especially with people like Kara." The squirrel runs off of Sobek and charges away without carrying any new messages.

I can almost feel smoke coming out of my ears. My eyes narrow on the golden dragon. "Sobek, are you coming back to guard the entrance, or what?" I plant my fists on my hips. "In fact, we should have been on our way by now, and it's because of you that we haven't started traveling yet."

Yes, ma'am! Sobek's chuckle continues to rumble through his ample belly.

I growl, "I can hear you, Sobek."

Chapter Eighteen

"So what were you two talking about?" I ask. "You and Ratatoskr seemed quite friendly. I thought he didn't speak to anyone unless he's delivering an insult."

An amused gleam passes through Sobek's eyes. *It was nothing that interesting.* He looks thoughtful for a moment then shakes his head. *No, just small chitchat.*

I grumble softly. "You're rather frustrating at times. Do you know that?"

Sobek bows mockingly. *I'm glad I could be of assistance.*

I huff. "You two suit each other."

We reach the cave and find our friends still asleep, the Valkyries curled against the warmth and protection of their dragons.

"Let's wake them. We have to go. You start with the dragons, and I'll wake the Valkyries."

Sobek's grin looks cunning. *With pleasure.*

Pausing, I raise an eyebrow at him. "You know, I have to say I don't remember you being so cheeky when I stayed with you in the dragon wastelands."

He shrugs. *I've relaxed around you. Back in the wastelands, I had to protect you. Now... well... you're just my sister's friend, perfectly capable of taking care of herself.*

"Nice! I thought you came on this trip to make sure your sister's friend stayed safe."

Sobek pokes Tanda with his nose, the prodding taking a few attempts before the red dragon opens her eyes. She climbs to her talons, nudging Britta in the process.

Starting on the right, I shake Hildr softly by the shoulder.

Slowly, she rolls over on all fours, eventually pushing herself up to standing, and stretches. Yawning, she rakes her fingers through her short red hair, pulling it into the spiky design she likes. "Is it time to go?"

Clasping Eir by the arm, I softly shake her. "There's enough moonlight to read the map. We should get going. I want to get out of this land as soon as possible."

Eir yawns and holds a hand over her mouth, eventually prying her eyes open. She wipes out the ducts then climbs onto Naga. "Let's get going.

I hope we don't get kidnapped by giants this time."

Britta climbs onto the saddle and hooks her feet into the stirrups. "I suggest we fly higher than the giants' reach this time."

Strapping my feet into Sobek's stirrups, I say, "That was the plan."

Britta turns to me. "Do you think you can see the land properly in the moonlight from that high up?"

"I think so. If not, then I'll fly lower with Sobek invisible, and you lot can stay above. If we have to use this method, I'll reappear now and then, and the dragons can communicate so that you know where we are."

After shrugging on the dragon-scale cloak, I pull the hood over my head, and the dragons pad softly toward the cave entrance. The frosty breeze brushes our skin, and moonlight bathes the icy landscape before us, giving it a fairy-tale appeal. The second we reach the exit, Sobek turns invisible.

"Wait here," I call to the others while scanning the area around the cave from the ground to the sky. "We're going to do a quick check to make sure all is clear and you can exit the cave safely." I stick my fingers under Sobek's scales just in front of the saddle, touching the soft, warm skin underneath. "Are you okay with that, Sobek?"

"Of course," Sobek says, sounding as though he's feigning confidence and importance.

His changing character throws me into uncertainty, and I frown. He's suddenly acting sensible and reliable. We lunge into the air, the beat of his massive wings jerking me as we climb into the sky. The increase of altitude brings a crispier cool breeze, and my eyes water in discomfort. My face stings, and any skin exposed to the elements turns numb after a few moments. The ground falls away underneath me, and in his invisible form, Sobek circles the area several times, surveying the cave and the other mountains within the vicinity.

After making certain that no threats lay hidden, we wind farther until something catches my eye in a corridor of the distant mountains. I pull on the reins, directing Sobek's head in that direction.

"Over that way, Sobek. I see movement."

I'm on it.

Tilting his wings, he steers us that direction, and I relax the pull on his reins, letting him take the lead. He keeps our altitude level for quite some time, his eye on the movement. Suddenly he dives toward the ground, and a scream stops behind my clenched teeth.

"What are you doing? We don't need to fly this

low to see what it is. We're flying in the danger zone."

We're invisible. He sounds conceited, making me want to slap him. *Whatever it is, it won't be able to see us.*

A growl sits in my throat, but I refuse to release it. It would probably just encourage him, knowing that his sudden dive set my nerves on edge. Our flight stabilizes as he glides, using the wind to his advantage as he captures it within his membranous wings. Eventually, we near the moving object, and we dip slightly closer to the ground, riding just over it. Sobek flaps his wings a few times, raising us higher, then circles the area twice.

I'm having trouble working out what I'm looking at. It appears to be an animal that I haven't seen before. "What is it?"

No idea. It must be an animal native to Jotunheim.

The thing scrambles around a tight spot, its face down as it devours something. Sobek sinks to a level just out of the animal's reach, gliding in a circular motion. It doesn't look up even though it might have felt the breeze from Sobek's wings. My impatience grows, and I yell. The animal looks up, and I'm confronted by a piglike nose. The rest of the body is covered with long white fur that spreads all the way down its legs, stopping at the trotters. The design of the animal is perfect for the cold weather in Jotunheim.

Satisfied, I say, "It looks like only a pig. It shouldn't be dangerous to us unless it has the temperament of a boar. Let's fly up. Let's go back to the others."

Yes, ma'am, Sobek says. *But we shouldn't get complacent. Maybe everything in this land is dangerous to us.*

"We'll keep an eye on everything."

Of course you will. The presumption returns to his voice.

I roll my eyes, not that he could see. "I didn't think your seriousness would last long. You seem to thrive on being cheeky." I push my mouth to one side. "And not always in a good way."

You're welcome, Sobek says. *This little trip would have been boring without me.*

"Yeah." I pile on the sarcasm. "Because rescuing my friends from frost giants isn't exciting at all."

In a few minutes, we return to our friends.

"We only found something like a wild pig. There don't seem to be any frost giants hanging around. However, while saying that, I suggest we keep away from anything that moves," I say.

Hildr's grip around her reins tightens. "Lead the way."

The dragons take to the sky and rise as planned until they are high enough to be out of the reach of any giants. Above the cloud cover, the moonlight shines on the map I pull from my cloak. I turn the map one way then the next, trying to find a location that reflects the markings on the map. "Thor's drawings are rough, certainly not the effort of an artist." I twist my mouth to the side. "But clear enough for recognizing landmarks. It's been several years since Thor and Tyr traveled here to retrieve Loki's three children—Jormungundr, Fenrir, and Hel—from Angrboda." I twist the map in another direction. "After looking at the drawings on the map and the landscape, it's possible that his memory has faded as well." I spot a set of mountains drawn on the map. "Thankfully, it might not have faded too much."

Britta moves next to me on Tanda's back. "I hate to be the bearer of bad news, but you know there's no guarantee that this is where the mother is going to be. No one, other than Loki, seems to know where she moved to after losing her children. She might have relocated to a completely different location."

Sobek scoffs. *Frost giants are creatures of habit. She'll be there.*

"How would you know?" I ask.

I just do.

I shake my head. "Somehow, that doesn't bring

me comfort. So let's hope she's still there." After finding a couple more bearings on the map, I roll it up and tuck it back into my cloak. "I think I have enough information. Let's go." I direct Sobek with the reins, and the others follow. The dragons fly in a diamond formation, Sobek leading the way and Naga tucked just behind in the middle.

Chapter Nineteen

After flying several leagues, Sobek and I turn invisible and drop below the clouds, and I pull out the map and study it in the moonlight. The wind whips at the edges of the parchment, threatening to rip it from my hands, and I tighten my hold. The last thing we need is for it to be lost in the wind. I study each section of the map. A sickness grows in my stomach as I struggle to find any of the landmarks.

Groaning in frustration, I say, "Pull up, Sobek. I need to find my bearings. I don't want to travel any farther until I'm sure we're going the right way."

Sobek makes us visible and circles the other dragons, giving me time as my companions' curious eyes observe me.

"I can't find where we are on the map. I need to reassess it for a moment," I say in answer to their unvoiced questions.

"Let me have a look." Britta holds out her hand, expectantly.

"The coast is clear of giants." I roll the map tight and hand it to her, refusing to release it until I'm certain she has a firm grasp.

We drop below the clouds and hover, waiting for Britta to test her navigation skills. Her brows furrow, and her lips flatten into a line as she pulls the map closer to her face, studying certain areas more closely than others. The dragons hover, waiting for her decision, occasionally watching her as she angles the map in new directions in the moonlight. Her frown deepens, and she peers over the side of Tanda, glancing past the hovering wings.

"Ah." She points down at the spot below her. "There it is." Her expression turns to excitement. "There's one of the icons. We're not far now." Then she points over to the right. "It's just a little farther that way."

A welcome relief washes over me. "Awesome! Can you lead the way?"

"Of course." Britta rolls up the map and tucks it into her jacket. "Follow us!" she calls over her shoulder before directing Tanda and leading the group in the right direction.

We remain high, just below the clouds. The hood drags off my head, pushed by the force of the wind.

White noise fills my ears as the wind thrums against my eardrums, making it hard to hear anything but its constant beat.

We pass several large buildings, and after having seen only a frosty countryside during my past visits, finding that the frost giants live in communities seems strange.

The moon begins its descent, aiming for the horizon in the west, and a rising shine on the far side indicates the sun, determined to start a new day. We pass several more buildings and aim for the cave where Thor and Tyr found Loki's children.

Britta slows Tanda, giving us time to reach their side. "The coast seems clear!"

"It seems that way," I agree. "But stay alert, just in case."

After a final circle around the mountains, we land not far from a cave resembling the one marked on the map. It doesn't look much different from the one we slept in except for a river flowing nearby, surrounded by greenery. After dismounting Sobek, I loosen the straps holding my cloak together. Although the wind still holds a chilliness, it isn't as cold as the temperatures we've encountered in Jotunheim before. I gape at the greenery and notice a thick tree trunk forking out into smaller branches covered in deep-green leaves. I run my fingers under some of the lower leaves, green tips flicking across my skin. "There's even a few trees in this area." I study the branches and leaves. "Some of those leaves appear to be like the ones on the World Tree."

Of course they do. Sobek shakes his head as though in disbelief. *The branches of Yggdrasil spread out wide even if you can't access the tunnel. If you're small enough, you'll be able to travel along the branches of the World Tree. They spread far among every realm. How do you think Ratatoskr finds all these people?*

"I've never thought about it."

Sobek shakes his head. *He can't run too far from the tree. He's only a small guy.*

"I hadn't really thought about it," I repeat. "I guess I assumed that he scurries the lands until he finds the person or creature he needs to talk to. That would be the best way to listen to rumors of where his target is residing." I shrug. "It's not like you can ask him these things."

Sobek snorts. *I think you're wrong about that. I find the little guy quite approachable.*

I shove a finger at his nose. "See. I thought you two had something going on." The soft flesh bends away as I jab it. Pulling away, I indicate another tree. "This tree looks different from the Yggdrasil."

Sobek shrugs, looking indifferent.

Grumbling to myself over his lack of response, I

gaze at the entrance of the cave. "Anyway… We must get going and do this quietly. She isn't expecting us." After taking a few quiet steps, I add, "I'm not sure if she's even here. But naturally, we need to eliminate as many risks as possible."

"Then I think it's best if we all gather our magic," Eir says, "and not rely on eloquence."

"That's a strange thing for you to say, Eir," Britta whispers. "Are you feeling all right?"

Eir frowns. "Yeah, Why?"

Britta feels for her sword, hanging by her leg, then her quiver on her back. The shafts rattle as she runs her fingers over the feathers. "You're usually against anything to do with hurting anything."

Eir groans and reties her long light-brown locks into a ponytail, securing all the loose wavy strands. "I know. I don't plan on hurting anyone, but I think it's wise to be prepared. We've already had enough excitement on the trip. At least if our magic is ready, it may give us enough to help us escape if needed."

I place a hand on Eir's shoulder, the soft leather in her black fighting uniform bending under my touch. "Whatever the reason, it is probably the best way to protect ourselves at the moment. Our tiny little swords or arrows against huge frost giants are just not enough."

My footsteps turn into tiptoeing as we slowly

enter the tunnel, doing our best keep our boots silent on the hard floor. Our breaths are shallow and soft, yet the sound reverberates back at us from the tunnel walls. The dragons' talons scrape on the stones, and I flinch at the loudness.

I whisper over my shoulder, "I think you dragons should stay here for now." When answered by confused looks, I continue, "Your talons are too loud, and the noise might alert her of us coming. Just remain alert in case we call for you. If there is anyone down at the end, we want to surprise them until we know what we're dealing with. We don't want to be ambushed the second we get down there."

The dragons plunk themselves on their haunches and wait, bored looks plastered on their scaled faces as we leave them behind.

"I have no idea where Angrboda lives," I say.

"Do you think there's a chance she'll be down here?" Eir's light-brown eyes are clouded with apprehension.

"To be honest, it would seem strange that she would remain here. I don't think I would like to remain in a place my children were taken from. It would be depressing."

The tunnel darkens, the deeper we travel. Beside me, Eir's leather uniform squeaks before I hear a sharp crack. A glow ignites in her hand, and a faint waft of smoke greets my nose.

I gasp. "You brought a flint striker! Way to go!"

A satisfied smile spreads across her face as she calls the flame to her open palm. The fire hovers over her hand, and she shoves the flint striker back into her fighting leathers. A soft incantation whispers through her lips, and the flame on her hand dances, jumping higher and growing in volume.

Hildr's eyes are wide, the whites shining in the light of the flame. "That's a cool little trick you've got there, Eir."

"We told you she was working on another type of magic, Hildr." Britta's face glows in the light next to Hildr. Despite her words, wonder covers her face. "This is one of the things she can do."

"It's one of the peaceful things I've been working on, while you've just focused on fighting and battle skills, Hildr." A simple matter-of-fact tone frames her words.

We push forward. The flame flickers over Eir's palm as we progress, each step drumming up a slight wind, causing it to continue dancing.

We progress toward the end of the tunnel, searching for the cave Thor described to me. My hopes dwindle as the width narrows without any sign of Angrboda and almost disintegrate when we run into a solid rock wall. It's the end of the cave.

With her palm leading the way, Eir circles the area, her flame illuminating the room, and flickers its light against the walls, revealing an empty cave.

Hildr's shoulders slump. "It looks as though it's a dead end."

"Where to now?" Britta asks.

"I don't know." I try to push down the frustration that chews on my nerves. "After we leave this cave, we'll circle the area, looking for somewhere that might resemble something that she lives in."

Suddenly, Drogon's voice enters our heads. *Ah, Valkyries… You might want to come out here. There's somebody that wants to see you.*

Chapter Twenty

Concerned glances pass between the other Valkyries and me, and we break into a run toward the entrance of the tunnel, all attempts to be silent smashed. The dragons' backs face us as they focus on something outside. Magic fires under my skin, loaded and waiting to be released, and my fingers twitch, longing to unleash my weapons.

We slow not far behind the dragons and cautiously approach their sides. Using Sobek as a shield, I duck behind a front leg and peer into the light.

Long brown leather pants cover towering muscled legs stand before us, the waistline hiding under a long tunic tied at the waist and cutting off midthigh. Leather straps with silver buckles dangle from the belt, and a silver sword sheath is suspended from the waistband. As it sways, its metal clangs against buckles and studs.

When I follow the long white hair falling past a waist in a thick braid, my mouth wants to fall open. A pale-blue giant stares down at us, her determined eyes focused on us from a face lined with blue zigzagging tattoos trickling down her cheeks. Something about them reminds me of some of Gilroma's tattoos even though the markings are different. Perhaps some of the strange dark elf's markings stemmed from the frost giants. I push aside the odd coincidence to focus.

Secured in a steady stance, a nocked arrow points directly at our small group, and the giant's blue fingers are poised, ready to release the string. I pull my attention past the fierce blue eyes and take in other features. Despite her size, her face is elegant, almost beautiful. As though sensing my wonder, she points the tip of the arrow directly at me, and I straighten. I feel incredibly small and insignificant, and I can't help wondering what such a large arrow would do to someone my size.

I silently whistle a puff of breath and steel my nerves. Without dropping my gaze, I secure my dragon-scale cape to cover more of my body. Yanking at the straps to tighten them in place, I hope the tough scales will withstand an arrow that size. Then I realize it doesn't matter. The pressure of something that big hitting my body, even through the cape, would pummel my organs and probably do too much damage. Gathering courage, I move slowly from around the security of Sobek's leg and approach her. Even though a fair distance still separates us, I crane my neck to focus on her eyes. They narrow, turning as hard as icicles as they glare down at me.

With each step I take, she adjusts her arrow to aim straight at me. I gulp, trying to swallow the lump stuck in my throat. My fingers fiddle nervously with the straps of my cloak, and I push my palms together, wrapping my fingers to secure them in place, in an effort to squash the hesitancy in my steps.

"Halt!" the frost giant calls. Her voice is strong and deep, almost as low as a male's.

My steps falter, and I do as instructed, forcing down my fear and staring straight into her face.

She lifts a blond eyebrow as though pleased with the result. "What do you want here? Why are there dragons here and four Valkyries?"

Bracing myself, I call out from the depth of my diaphragm, trying to make my voice bigger. "We're searching for someone."

Her brows furrow, and suspicion creeps through her expression.

I continue, "We come in peace. We do not want to cause any trouble."

The female frost giant huffs a laugh, sounding

unconvinced. "When do Valkyries ever come in peace?" Her face turns cunning. "If you come in search of my children, then you're out of luck. They were taken by the gods. You should know that, for they were taken to Asgard and distributed to different realms." She raises her chin. "There's been nobody residing in this cave since my children were taken. There is no reason for you to be here."

My jaw drops. She said her "children." I brace myself for mockery, but to me, that seems the only explanation. "Angrboda?"

Her face twists before it quickly flattens again.

"Is that you?" I try again.

Something firm presses me from behind, and golden scales catch the corner of my eyes. Sobek leans over me, and hot breath falls over my shoulders. His eyes remain fixed on the female giant.

His face beams, almost dreamy, as he says softly, "Can't you tell? Look at those gorgeous blue eyes."

I nudge him with my elbow. "Sobek. Get a hold of yourself." Afraid to take my eyes off the giant for too long, I return my gaze just in time to see her determination waver with a moment of softness in her blue eyes as they focus on Sobek.

Her gaze returns to steel as her attention turns toward me. "Who wants to know?"

Placing a hand slowly on my chest, I say, "I'm

Kara, a Valkyrie and mostly a peacekeeper. These are my wingless colleagues and their dragon companions." I wave a hand around the group. "We just want to talk to Angrboda."

"Then you're looking for me. I am Angrboda, also known as Loki's mistress." Her brow furrows, pushing together the blue lines that streak down her forehead. "Why would you be looking for me?" Keeping the arrow nocked, she drops the point away from us.

Eir moves forward, placing her peaceful face in the spotlight. "We just want to ask you some questions."

She chuckles and sits on the ground, crossing her long thin legs. Even at her reduced height, she still towers over us. "What sort of questions would drag you into the dangers of Jotunheim just to search for me?"

Confused by the sudden ease infused in her manner, I twiddle my thumbs behind my back. "Do you have any pull on how your children behave? We were wondering… and hoping… if you could control your children a little bit."

"Why?" She raises her nose, looking slightly annoyed yet amused. "They're teenagers. Nobody can control teenagers."

"Are you saying you have no influence over your children?" Britta asks.

Angrboda's blue eyes flash a warning as she stares Britta down. "For one, the gods pinched my children years ago. They haven't been in my care for quite some time." She flicks a dismissive hand out to the side. "Why would you think they would listen to me after all this time? Can't the gods control them?" She eyes us individually. "If they took my children, they should learn how to control them."

Eir's places a hand on the giant's knee. "Did you want them back?" A strange, hopeful sound fills her voice. "Perhaps they would be more settled if they came back to their mother."

The mistress's laugh is so high-pitched that I have to cover my ears. She slaps a hand against the ground, and smaller stones around her jump and clatter a short distance. "That's a funny one." She thumps the ground a few more times. "As if I want my wayward children back. They have a power that you will never understand. Besides, have you not heard? They are monsters."

Annoyance whirls and raises its ugly head within me, and I push it down with a frown. "Yes. That is why we're here. We hoped that you would help us control them. It is essential for Asgard, and for many other realms, that they are controlled."

Hildr stands by my side and crosses her arms. "How did you manage to have three completely unique monsters with one god, anyway?"

The mistress slaps a hand over her mouth as she chuckles. Eventually, her laughter grows so loud that she can't contain it anymore. Rocking back, she holds her stomach and laughs boisterously until she finally regains her composure. Wiping the laughter tears from her eyes, she sits up and stares down at Hildr before gazing at all the Valkyries. "You are young Valkyries, yes?"

Hildr stands on one leg, her arms remaining crossed. "We are still young as far as a Valkyrie is concerned. What is your point?"

"That perhaps you are too young to understand."

When we stare at her with confusion, she continues, speaking slowly and emphasizing her words, "Loki is a shape-shifter. Think about it." When our expressions don't change, she adds, "Perhaps you should go back to the academy and learn some Baby-making 101 skills."

I feel my cheeks redden and turn away, trying to hide my face. An awkward silence taints the air, broken by the clearing of throats then Angrboda's laughter.

In one way, I'm glad for the distraction of her laughter so I can regain my composure. When she finally quiets down, I add, "We need all the help we can get to stop your children. They have been causing trouble ever since they learned of their father's demise."

"Ha. Then let him go." She says this so simply and matter-of-factly that it shocks me.

I take several steps back, running into Sobek. "We can't just do that. He has caused so much trouble on Asgard, and he's extremely deceitful."

"But my suggestion may be your only answer." Placing her palms on her knees, she leans forward as though plotting a conspiracy. "Or have you lost him?" Her eyes narrow on me. "I've heard rumors that he has escaped. Is that what you're not telling me?"

My gaze drops to the ground, and I fiddle with my fingers before pulling my gaze back up. "Yes, it's true. He's no longer held in captivity by the gods. He has run away somewhere."

Chapter Twenty-One

After recovering from my embarrassment over my failure, I look up. Angrboda is beautiful compared to the other frost giants I've seen, and I understand to some degree how Loki could fall for her. After all, he was also part frost giant and a shape-shifter. However, I didn't want to think about how he managed to create different types of monsters as children. They aren't the only unusual children Loki sired. I heard that Odin's eight-legged horse, Sleipnir, was created because Loki shape-shifted into a horse to lure another away and ended up having a baby with it.

"Then can you help us to find Loki?" I stare up at her with hope. "I must redeem myself before the gods."

She rests her elbows on her knees and leans forward, staring down at me. Even though her movement isn't aggressive or threatening, her massive form towering over me is daunting and makes me feel small and insignificant.

She raises a white eyebrow. "Have you not found him yet?"

Sobek makes a funny sound in his throat. Glancing at him, I'm surprised by his expression. It appears to be riddled with love and adoration, his eyes soft as he gazes at Angrboda, his face about to melt with passion. He said she was pretty, but this is ridiculous.

Shaking my head, I return my attention to the mistress. "No. I haven't found him. If I don't find him, I'll be in lots of trouble."

Amusement grows on her face.

My jaw drops. "Do you know where he is?"

"Maybe."

"I know I can't expect any favors from you, but if you tell me where he is, I can rectify my mistake, and I'll make sure he'll get treated better than last time."

Still towering over me, she gazes at me intensely with her big blue eyes then over my shoulder, taking in my golden mount, before returning to me. "No. I cannot help you find him. You must rectify what you have done on your own. If he is chained up, I will never get to see him, and that is simply not good enough." She sits straight. "But if you do capture him and make sure he is treated nicer than before, I may put in a good word for you with our children." She crosses her arms and gazes at me curiously. "You know he's a shape-shifter, right?"

"Of course I know that," I say, almost insulted. "Besides, you mentioned that only a little while ago, plus I've seen him in many shapes since I've known him."

The edges of her mouth tilt up in a smirk. "Well then, you know he can take on any form. So good luck with that."

I resist the urge to stomp my foot and glare at her. "We have traveled a long way and dealt with much danger to ask you these questions. Can you please help us out slightly? At least give us some help with the children."

"Hmm. You have been somewhat pleasant to talk to even though you're a Valkyrie and work for Asgard." She rests her chin on a hand. "I guess I'll think about talking to the children anyway."

I breathe the words, "Thank you." Then I add, "Any help will be appreciated. This isn't only for Asgard's safety."

"I don't know if my chats will be that helpful." Levering herself off the ground, she stands then bends to look at me. "Seeing you know that Loki is a shape-shifter, you must know that he could be anywhere... or anyone. Perhaps he is closer than you think." She turns to leave and calls over her shoulder, "Oh, and take note, if you follow me, I will kill you."

From the warning in her eye, I wasn't going to test her threat.

"And that goes for your friends and the dragons too." After facing us, her glare lands on each of us and finishes with Sobek. She bends over and frames his golden snout in her hand.

I move back, observing her. It's such an unusual thing to do. Sobek's scales glimmer in the light of the early morning.

Lightly, she shakes his jaw, gazing straight into his golden-brown eyes. "You're a beautiful dragon, aren't you?" She kisses his forehead then strokes his body from the top of his head, down his back, avoiding the saddle.

Sobek moves into the stroke, his face soft with adoration.

Her eyes land on me, observing my surprised expression with humor. "Emperor dragons are magnificent creatures, aren't they?" Without waiting for an answer, she straightens.

A thunderous rumble breaks the silence, and a crack of lightning follows, forking into silver lines and splitting the sky. Surprised, I stare at the icy blue sky. The clouds there didn't indicate a storm.

Angrboda growls, and the tunnel shakes with a

different kind of thunder. She glowers at me. "You said you come in peace."

"We do," I stammer.

She extends her long arm at the sky. "Then why did you bring the horrid god of thunder?"

"What?" Open-mouthed, I stare at the sky again, and another rumble of thunder sends vibrations through the ground, followed by another crack of lightning, forking in two directions.

"You have lied to me. I will not help you now. There is no chance I'll help you find Loki, nor will I try to convince our children to stop attacking Asgard and your gods."

I try to argue. "But—"

My words are cut off by the sound of sliding metal as she unsheathes her sword.

Lightning forks from the sky, hitting the ground only a few yards away, and everyone in the cave jumps, but no one as much as Angrboda. A determined snarl replaces all pleasantness in her face. She repositions her feet in a firm stance and raises her sword.

Suddenly, something shoots from the sky and lands with a thud right where the last bolt of lightning hit. The ground shakes from the impact, and a figure of a man rises from a squat. Dressed in brown leather topped with a tunic and a long fur cloak, Thor stands with hair burning red in the sun's light, an enormous hammer in hand.

"Wow!" Hildr exclaims. "That never grows old." The sound of metal slides as she yanks her sword out of her sheath.

I grasp her arm. "Wait!" When met with a frown, I continue, "I don't understand why he is here. Maybe he's just here for a chat."

"Uh, I don't know how you don't already know this, but if Thor arrives in this fashion, it's always because he's coming to fight." Hildr indicates Angrboda. "Even she knows this."

"But why would he be coming to fight when there is no need to?" I ask. "We weren't in danger, and she was sort of cooperating."

Angrboda charges for the god of thunder, her large legs covering the ground in seconds, her sword held high. Casually walking her way, Thor holds Mjollnir to the sky, and lightning forks from the hammer into the sky and hits the ground right before Angrboda's next footstep.

She grinds to a halt, her foot raised, before placing it back down cautiously. "You'll pay for that."

"And you'll pay for mistreating my Valkyrie and her companions." Thor swings the hammer and releases it. It charges straight at Angrboda, slamming into her torso and sending her reeling backward past the cave entrance. Pebbles fall from the ceiling of the cave as a loud thud rings out and the ground shakes. Thor holds out his hand, beckoning Mjollnir, and is rewarded only moments later when the hammer's helve slaps into his palm.

What is he doing? Concern fills Sobek's voice.

"I don't know." I shake my head. "I don't know why he's here. It doesn't make sense."

"We have to stop him." Eir shifts to leave the cave.

I grab her arm. "I'll do it."

Solemnly, she nods.

Pebbles sting my head again as heavy footsteps charge past the entrance. A loud cry cuts the silence as Angrboda swings her sword at Thor.

Thor ducks, pivots, and releases Mjollnir in the opposite direction, directing it with his hand to fly back with added momentum directly at Angrboda. It slams into her stomach again and pushes her several yards away from him before landing in his extended palm.

His boots crunch on the realm's stony surface as he paces toward the female frost giant.

I charge out of the cave, waving my hands. "Thor. Stop!"

His expression is curious when his eyes land on me.

"Look!" I wave my hands, pointing to my body.

"I'm unharmed." I indicate the cave. "My companions are safe. Angrboda was not attacking us."

He frowns. "But Ratat—" Understanding fills his face. "Why that dirty little rat."

I groan. Clearly, he has been misinformed.

With a smile, I say, "Well, it's good to know that you will turn up if you hear I'm in trouble."

"That is true, Kara. But this time, it appears I've made a grave mistake." He nods to the giantess, who is rising with a promise to kill written on her face. "My apologies, Angrboda. I was misled." Twirling his arm, he swings his hammer and lets himself be carried away by the momentum, out of sight.

Taking in Angrboda's face, I groan. "Thor thought you were hurting us. I'm sorry."

Completely risen to her feet, she growls and leers over me. "Your apology for your stupid god is not accepted. You can forget receiving any help from me. You're lucky I don't kill the lot of you now. You're nothing to me." She straightens and stomps off.

When she's gone, I groan. "What are we going to do now?"

"That was a waste of a mission," Eir says.

"You don't have to tell me." I check the straps of the saddle on Sobek, tightening any loose belts. "We came all of this way for nothing. She's not going to help us the slightest bit, even if it is also for other realms." I expel a massive groan and stomp my feet. "Now I have to return to Asgard with nothing. This is embarrassing and a disappointment."

Britta rests a hand on my shoulder. "At least you can blame Thor if he gets testy over a fruitless trip."

Hildr slides her sword back into its sheath. "That has some truth to it. She was going to cooperate with you a little bit. I don't know if it would have been much help."

"I guess. Really though, I don't think she was going to help us. It was going to be a pretty useless trip."

It wasn't all bad. Sobek sits next to me, his eyes soft with admiration. *After all, you got to meet Loki's mistress.*

"Sobek. Get over it. She's just a frost giant in a female form, an enemy of Asgard, Valkyries, and dragons alike." I shake my head. "No amount of beauty is worth that much trouble."

But I'm sure she liked me. Didn't you see? Sobek swoons. *She even kissed me and rubbed my body.*

"Probably because you stared at her with adoring eyes," I say. "You looked like you were about to smother her with love kisses."

Well, she is gorgeous. Sobek drools.

I groan. "Let's go. We didn't get anywhere, and I want to go home to contemplate my next move before Odin finds out." Sobek sinks onto his chest, and I yank myself up onto the saddle. "Take me straight home, please, Sobek." My body slumps over in defeat. "Take me home as quickly as possible. I want to go back to safety and away from this dreaded land filled with frost giants."

Chapter Twenty-Two

Sobek extends his wings, and we glide down to the apartment Hildr, Britta, Eir, and I share. The golden dragon lands on the ground with a soft thud. I climb off and immediately unbuckle the straps. With a slight tug, the saddle slides off his back and down his side. Hunkering down, I drag it to the apartment as the three soft thuds from the other dragons sound behind me.

"This is it." I circle to the front of Sobek and face him. "Thank you for your assistance, Sobek." I purse my lips. "It's been interesting, but I couldn't have done it without you."

Sobek puffs out his chest. *I know you couldn't have done it without me. And you would've been bored if I didn't come.*

"Without Elan, that might have been true... although I'm sure I'd find all dragons interesting." I stop myself, realizing I sound ungrateful. "Still, thank you for taking me." As the other three Valkyries remove the saddles from their dragons, I rest a hand on his snout. "Are you going to visit your sister now?"

No. We've only been gone for about two days. I'm sure she's fine, and I need to get back to Mother to tell her that my sister is okay. When I gaze at him in disbelief, he continues, *We're not that close, you know.*

I shrug. "I'm going to see Elan as soon as I can. I want to see how she's doing. Don't you want to come with me?"

I'll see her next time. Sobek pushes off into the sky, flapping his enormous wings. Dust and dirt billow from the ground, surrounding me. Sheltering my eyes, I blink up at his spectacular form.

"Elan's brother is rather… interesting." Eir stands beside me, her chest heaving as she catches her breath after having moved the saddle.

I cross my arms. "You don't need to tell me. Elan has her humor, and it's often mischievous, yet it's different from Sobek's. Even so, I couldn't have made the trip without him."

Hildr and Britta pull at their dragons' saddles, which land on the ground with a thud. A trail cuts through the dirt as they drag them toward the apartment, next to mine, exhaustion riddling their faces.

"What are you guys going to do now?" I ask.

"I'm beat," Britta says. "I'm going to rest for a while."

"Me too." Hildr's face looks drawn, making her red hair seem brighter. "It was a tiring trip. I'm going to rest for a while, seeing nothing urgent needs addressing."

Drogon and Tanda curl up near the apartment.

Eir strokes the side of Naga's face as he nudges into her hand. "I'm going to stay with Naga for a while. Are you happy to rest here with me for a while, Naga?"

Naga nods and slumps to his stomach, and Eir stretches within his forearms, leaning back against his chest. She presses her palms together and nestles her hands under her face, almost as though she's ready to curl up and go to sleep. She looks at me with sleepy eyes. "Are you going to visit Elan, Kara?"

"Yes. I want to see if she's okay. I'm keen to find out if she is feeling any better."

Eir yawns. "Okay. I'll see you later, then."

Naga circles his head around her, resting his chin on his front talons. The blue dragon and my peaceful friend look adorable curled up together.

The trip has been a big one, and I'm not surprised the others need rest. Even though I'm exhausted, my rest can wait until after I've seen Elan. Not bothering to remove my quiver and sword, I take off to see her.

I'm so used to the weapons being on my back that I'm almost oblivious to the added weight.

When I reach the academy, I pause to catch my breath, only to find the spot where I left Elan empty. My heart speeds up, worry niggling at my core until I remind myself that she's probably healed and moved on.

A shadow passes over me as a yellow dragon glides over the academy and circles back to the training field. Legs dangle over its sides, the rider sitting firm, not flopping from side to side, unlike the last time I saw them. A few seconds later, another shadow passes over as the massive form of a dragon flips and golden scales glimmer in the sunshine. My heart leaps with joy. I would recognize that dragon anywhere. Elan glides behind the yellow dragon and rider. She must be helping them learn.

With a smile, I immediately sprint to the dragon rider's training field, ignoring the screams of protest from my exhausted body. Nothing is going to hold me back from seeing my beautiful golden dragon and best friend.

The yellow dragon lands smoothly, and Elan follows her. Even though I'm not included in Elan's projected words, I can see the excitement in her reactions as she dances on her back feet and extends her wings. Joy beams from her golden face as she communicates with the yellow dragon and its rider.

The wingless Valkyrie tucks a hand underneath the yellow scales, connecting with the dragon's soft flesh and expressing the growing trust between the dragon and its rider. As I approach from the side, I can see a broad smile on the Valkyrie's face. The improvement is remarkable, with a little guidance.

My running footsteps alert Elan's sharp dragon ears of my approach. She spins, her face stern until she catches sight of me and flashes a toothy grin.

Kara! You got home okay! She rears, and her talons move in a happy dance before she charges forward, not slowing until I slam into her nose. I grunt from the force and wrap my arms around her.

Before I can speak, the other dragon rider sneaks up behind Elan, her yellow dragon following. She runs her fingers through her dark shoulder-length hair, looking almost bashful. "Thank you, Elan. We're going to leave you to catch up with Kara. Thank you so much for your help," she repeats before turning to lead her dragon away without waiting for an answer.

Anytime! Elan calls after her, with a voice full of enthusiasm. *I'll see you later.* As they disappear into the distance, she turns her attention back to me. Her beautiful golden membranous wings spread with excitement and wrap around me.

My heart melts with satisfaction. "It's so good to see you up and about, Elan. You must be feeling better." I pull back. "Look at you."

Her chest puffs out. *Of course I'm feeling better. My best Valkyrie friend has returned, and she's in one piece. Which dragon did you take?* She peers from under a raised scaly eyebrow.

I chuckle. "You're not going to believe it."

Believe what? she asks. *What am I not going to believe?*

"Well, Sobek dropped by just after I saw you, and he offered to take me. He said he was checking to see if you're okay so that he could pass the news on to your mother. It had been a while since I talked to him. I didn't know he had such a weird sense of humor. I didn't notice that when I was with him in the dragon wastelands." I gaze up at her face, surprised to see a frown scrunched into her dragon scales. "What's wrong?"

What do you mean by Sobek?

My jaw drops. "Your brother, of course. Your brother offered to take me to Jotunheim. He was the one that took me all the way there and back." I frown up at her confused face.

And when did you get back?

"Just a few minutes ago. Why? I came straight here."

Elan's face is grim. *Sobek visited me early this morning.*

I gape at her. "What do you mean?"

It's simple. My brother dropped in early this morning to see if I was okay. He brought me some food and had a quick chat with me before returning to the wastelands.

Frowning, I spread my hands out at my side. "But Sobek was with me."

Elan shakes her head, her eyes somber.

"Then who took me to Jotunheim?"

She drops down to her front talons and lies on her stomach, leveling her eyes with mine. *Who is an expert shape-shifter that can take on any form he chooses?*

My knees buckle beneath me, and I flop to the ground, my legs crossed. The answer escapes in a hissed whisper. "Loki!"

Elan nods, slow and melancholy.

I flop onto my back and groan, ignoring the uncomfortable weapons rattling underneath me. "How did I not get it? It makes so much sense now. The unusual humor, the mischief, the ogling over the mistress." Growling, I hit the ground with my fist. "I'm so mad at myself. Loki was literally within my reach the whole time. No wonder the dreaded Ratatoskr was a little brat. He knew it was Loki. He even told me that Loki was closer than I thought. The mistress said the same thing." I slam my palm on my forehead. "How could I be so stupid?" I groan loudly before sitting upright and grasping Elan's nose in both hands, resting my forehead on her snout. Long dark hair shields both sides of my face from the world around me, and my focus narrows on my stupidity. "No wonder he didn't land to say hello to you. You would have known it was him because of the way he acted."

It's a strong possibility, yes. Elan huffs hot steam, which warms my body. *Don't beat yourself up so much. He is a master of disguise and a trickster. We will get him. Don't worry.*

After sucking in a big breath, I ask, "Can you at least tell me—have Loki's children stopped attacking Asgard and causing mischief since his escape?"

It's only been about two days since you left. I haven't heard anything much. I believe the gods are still trying to make a chain strong enough to secure Fenrir. He's been acting up, but I think that's mainly because he's an aggravated teenager. It's only threatening because he's so big. As per usual, the Midgard Serpent is always causing mischief, but nothing more than usual. As for Hel, I don't know. I haven't seen anything other than the lava monster coming up from Helheim to cause damage to Asgard.

From behind Elan, I hear a strange sound, and I push against her scales, gazing over her body. Instantly, I jump to my feet. "Get up, Elan! I thought you said nothing was coming up from Helheim. Get up!" I yell again.

Elan springs to her feet, but she's too late.

A large black hand scoops down and secures her and me within its grasp. The dark claw closes around us, pushing us together. I peer through the cracks between digits, my face pressed against the black forms, smothered in a heat warmer than a normal hand. My eyes widen as fear fastens a hard knot of helplessness in my stomach. Peering down at us secured in this grasp are two eyes set in a coal-like exterior, the contents burning red and hot like lava.

The End

~~~~~

If you enjoyed this book, please takes a few minutes of your time to review it on Amazon. Reviews help to grow my readership.

Entrapment: Book 3 - On Amazon soon

ACKNOWLEDGMENTS

Thank you to all of the creators of literature and websites who have spent time writing about Norse Mythology. Even though at times there has been contradicting information, it has been an interesting study. After all, of course a goat produces mead, and a dragon gnaws at the roots of the Yggdrasil, unhindered, threatening the existence of the nine realms attached to the world tree. Plus, there are many other "believable" tales told.

Norse mythology is such an impressive set of tales that I have incorporated some and invented others to create Kara and Elan's story.

I am touched by the enormous amount of support I have received from my immediate family. My husband has been a helpful first reader and, at times, been an excellent motivator, with hints of ideas to help me through the blanks. The support from my three sons has also been overwhelming. They have spent years putting up with my head in the clouds, thinking about the next plot twist or story, along with many hours spent working on my books and keeping in touch with my readers.

A big thank you to my extended family, who support me being a book enthusiast.

A huge thank you to my editor, Kelly Reed, her editing and writing tips, and my Proofreader, Kristina B, for picking up the things we missed.

Thank you to all of my readers who have loved my work, and continue to read my stories.

Supernatural Evolvement Series

(Associated with the Afterlife Series)

WITCH'S LEGACY (Prequel)

AALIYAH

~~~~~

Young Adult Norse Mythology Fantasy

Valkyrie Academy Dragon Alliance

MARKED

CHOSEN

VANISHED

SCORNED

INFLICTED

EMPOWERED

AMBUSHED

WARNED

ABDUCTED

BESIEGED

DECEIVED

Thor's Dragon Rider

SAFEGUARD

PURSUIT

ENTRAPMENT

Get updates & notifications of giveaways

Would you like a FREE ebook?

Click here to get started: FREE copy of Marked or go to
https://dl.bookfunnel.com/f4cm1zh2qb

Through this link you can sign up for my newsletter and
receive a FREE copy of Marked plus updates about my
fantasy books, sales and notification of giveaways.

ABOUT THE AUTHOR

Katrina is a best-selling author of young adult fantasy and middle grade/tween novels. Her novels incorporate action, heart and an intriguing plot.

She resides in Queensland, Australia. Her three teenage boys and husband for over twenty years treat her like a princess. Unfortunately though, this princess still has to do domestic chores.

From a very young age, she has been a very creative person and has spent many years travelling the world and observing many different personalities and cultures. Her favourite personalities have been the strange ones, yet the ones under the radar also hold a place in her heart.

Katrina's online home is at www.katrinacopebooks.com
    You can connect with Katrina on:
    Facebook Group

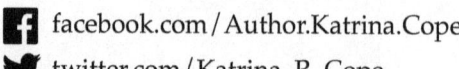

facebook.com/Author.Katrina.Cope

twitter.com/Katrina_R_Cope

instagram.com/katrina_cope_author

pinterest.com/katrinacope56

bookbub.com/profile/katrina-cope

www.ingramcontent.com/pod-product-compliance
Lightning Source LLC
Chambersburg PA
CBHW021959130726
47903CB00014B/2464